SECOND CHANCE

Danielle Steel

CORGI BOOKS

SECOND CHANCE
A CORGI BOOK : 0 552 14856 3

Originally published in Great Britain by Bantam Press,
a division of Transworld Publishers

PRINTING HISTORY
Bantam Press edition published 2004
Corgi edition published 2005

1 3 5 7 9 10 8 6 4 2

Set in 11/12.5pt Sabon by
Falcon Oast Graphic Art Ltd.

Corgi Books are published by Transworld Publishers,
61–63 Uxbridge Road, London W5 5SA,
a division of The Random House Group Ltd,
in Australia by Random House Australia (Pty) Ltd,
20 Alfred Street, Milsons Point, Sydney, NSW 2061, Australia,
in New Zealand by Random House New Zealand Ltd,
18 Poland Road, Glenfield, Auckland 10, New Zealand
and in South Africa by Random House (Pty) Ltd,
Endulini, 5a Jubilee Road, Parktown 2193, South Africa.

Printed and bound in Germany by
GGP Media GmbH, Poessneck.

Papers used by Transworld Publishers are natural, recyclable
products made from wood grown in sustainable forests. The
manufacturing processes conform to the environmental
regulations of the country of origin.

SECOND CHANCE

Also by Danielle Steel

* Published outside the UK under the title
PASSION'S PROMISE

To the lucky few who get a second chance,
and make it work.
And to my wonderful, wonderful children,
Trevor, Todd, Beatrix, Nick, Samantha,
Victoria, Vanessa, Maxx and Zara,
who are my reason for living,
and the joy of my life,

with all my love,
d.s.

We are all seeking that special person who is right for us. But if you've been through enough relationships, you begin to suspect there's no right person, just different flavors of wrong.

Why is this? Because you yourself are wrong in some way, and you seek out partners who are wrong in some complementary way. But it takes a lot of living to grow fully into your own wrongness. It isn't until you finally run up against your deepest demons – your unsolvable problems – the ones that make you who you truly are – that you're ready to find a lifelong mate. Only then do you finally know what you are looking for.

You are looking for the wrong person. But not just any wrong person: the 'right' wrong person – someone you lovingly gaze upon and think, 'This is the problem I want to have.'

I will find that special person who is wrong for me in just the right way.

—Andrew Boyd
Daily Afflictions

SECOND CHANCE

1

The air-conditioning had just stopped working in the offices of *Chic* magazine on a blisteringly hot June day in New York. It was their second brownout of the day, and Fiona Monaghan looked as if she were ready to kill someone as she strode into her office after being trapped in the elevator for twenty minutes. The same thing had happened to her the day before. Just getting out of the cab on the way back from lunch at the Four Seasons made her feel as though the air had been sucked out of her lungs. She was leaving for Paris in two weeks – if she lived that long. Days like this were enough to make anyone hate New York, but in spite of the heat and the aggravation, Fiona loved everything about living there. The people, the atmosphere, the restaurants, the theater, the avalanche of culture and excitement everywhere – even the brownstone on East Seventy-fourth Street that she had nearly bank-rupted herself to buy ten years ago. She had spent every penny she had on remodeling it. It was stylish and exquisite, a symbol of everything she was and had become.

At forty-two, she had spent a lifetime becoming Fiona Monaghan, a woman men admired and women envied, and came to love when they knew her well and she was their friend. If pressed, she could be a fearsome opponent. But even those who disliked her had to admit they respected her. She was a woman of power, passion, and integrity, and she would fight to the death for a cause she believed in, or a person she had promised to support. She never broke a promise, and when she gave her word, you knew you could count on her. She looked like Katharine Hepburn with a little dash of Rita Hayworth, she was tall and lean with bright red hair and big green eyes that flashed with either delight or rage. Those who met Fiona Monaghan never forgot her, and in her fiefdom she was all knowing, all seeing, all powerful, and all caring. She loved her job above all else, and had fought hard to get it. She had never married, never wanted to, and although she loved children, she never wanted any of her own. She had enough on her plate as it was. She had been the editor-in-chief of *Chic* magazine for six years, and as such she was an icon in the fashion world.

She had a full personal life as well. She had had an affair with a married man, and a relationship with a man she had lived with for eight years. Before that, she had dated randomly, usually artists or writers, but she had been alone now for a year and a half. The married lover was a British architect who commuted between London, Hong Kong, and New York. And the man she had lived with was a conductor, and had left her to marry and have children, and was living in Chicago now, which Fiona considered a fate worse than death. Fiona thought New York was the hub of the civilized world. She would have lived in London or Paris, but nowhere else. She and the conductor had remained good friends. He had come before the architect, whom she had left when the affair got too complicated and he threatened to leave his wife for her. She didn't want to marry him, or anyone. She hadn't wanted to marry the conductor either, although he had asked her repeatedly. Marriage always seemed too high-risk to her, she would have preferred to do a high-wire act in the circus than risk marriage, and she warned men of that. Marriage was never an option for her.

Her own childhood had been hard enough to convince her that she didn't want to risk that kind of pain for anyone. Her father had abandoned her mother when her mother was twenty-five and she was three. Her mother had attempted two more marriages to men Fiona hated, both were drunks, as her father had been. She never saw her father again after he left, nor his family, and knew only that he had died when she was fourteen. And her mother had died when she was in college. Fiona had no siblings, no known relatives. She was alone in the world by the time she was twenty, graduated from Wellesley, and made it on her own after that. She crawled her way up the ladder in minor fashion magazines and landed at *Chic* by the time she was twenty-nine. Seven years later, she became editor-in-chief, and the rest was history. Fiona was a legend by the time she was thirty-five, and the most powerful female magazine editor in the country at forty.

Fiona had nearly infallible judgment, an unfailing sense for fashion and what would work, and a head for business that everyone she worked with admired. And more than that, she had courage. She wasn't afraid to take risks, except in her love life. In that arena she took none at all, and had no need to. She wasn't afraid to be alone, and in the past year and a half she had come to prefer it. She was never really alone anyway, she was constantly surrounded by photographers, assistants, designers, models, artists, and a flock of hangers-on. She had a full calendar and an active social life and a host of interesting friends. She always said that it wouldn't bother her if she never lived with anyone again. She didn't have room in her closets anyway, and had no desire to make room for anyone. She had enough responsibilities at the magazine, without wanting to be responsible to or for a man as well. Fiona Monaghan had a breathtakingly full life, and she loved all of it. She had a high tolerance for, and a slight addiction to, confusion, excitement, and chaos.

She was wearing a long narrow black silk skirt that fell in tiny pleats from her waist, as she walked off the elevator she'd been trapped in for twenty minutes, on her way back from lunch. She wore a white peasant blouse with it, off her shoulders, with her long red hair swept up in a loose knot. Her only piece of jewelry was a huge turquoise bracelet that nearly devoured her wrist and was the envy of all who saw it. It had been made for her by David Webb. She was wearing high-heeled black Manolo Blahnik sandals, an oversize red alligator Fendi bag, and the entire combination of accessories and long, clean lines gave an impression of inimitable elegance and style. Fiona was as dazzling as any of the models they photographed, she was older but just as beautiful, although her looks meant nothing to her. She never traded on sex appeal or artifice, she was far more interested in the soul and the mind, both of which shone through her deep green eyes. She was thinking about the cover for the September issue, as she sat down at her desk, kicked off her sandals, and picked up the phone. There was a new young designer in Paris she wanted one of her young assistant editors to research and pursue. Fiona was always on a mission of some kind, it took a flock of underlings and minions to keep up with her, and she was feared as much as she was admired. You had to move fast to match her pace, and she had no patience for slackers, shirkers, or fools. Everyone at *Chic* knew that when Fiona shined the spotlight on you, you'd better be able to come up with the goods, or else.

Her secretary buzzed her ten minutes later to remind her that John Anderson was coming in to see her in half an hour, and she groaned. She had forgotten the appointment, and between the heat, the lack of air-conditioning, and the interlude in the elevator, she wasn't in the mood. He was the head of the new ad agency they'd hired, it was a solid old firm that, thanks to him, had come up with some exciting new ideas. It had been her decision to make the switch, and she had met nearly everyone in the agency but him. Their work and their track record spoke for itself. The meeting was merely a matter of form to meet each other. He had been reorganizing the London office when she decided to hire the firm, and now that he was back in town, they had agreed to meet. He had suggested lunch, but she didn't have time, so she'd suggested he come to her office, intending to keep it brief.

She returned half a dozen calls before the meeting, and Adrian Wicks, her most important editor, dropped in for five minutes to discuss the couture shows in Paris with her. Adrian was a tall, thin, stylish, somewhat effeminate black man who had been a designer himself for a few years before he came to *Chic*. He was as smart as she was, which she loved. Adrian was a graduate of Yale, had a master's in journalism from Columbia, worked as a designer, and had finally landed at *Chic*, and together they were an impressive team. He was her right arm for the last five years. He was as dark as she was pale, as addicted to fashion as she, and as passionate about his ideas and the magazine as Fiona. In addition, he was her best friend. She invited him to join the meeting with John Anderson, but he was meeting with a designer at three, and just as Adrian left her office, her secretary told her that Mr. Anderson had arrived, and Fiona asked her to show him in.

As Fiona looked across her desk to the doorway, she watched John Anderson walk in, and came around her desk to greet him. She smiled as their eyes met, and each took the other's measure. He was a tall, powerfully built man with impeccably groomed white hair, bright blue eyes, and a youthful face and demeanor. He was as conservative as she was flamboyant. She knew from his biographical material, and mutual friends, that he was a widower, he had just turned fifty, and he had an M.B.A. from Harvard. She also knew he had two daughters in college, one at Brown and the other at Princeton. Fiona always remembered personal details, she found them interesting, and sometimes useful to help her know who she was dealing with.

'Thank you for coming over,' she said pleasantly as they stood eyeing each other. She was nearly as tall as he was in the towering Blahnik heels she had slipped back on before she came to greet him.

17

The rest of the time, she loved walking around her office barefoot. She said it helped her think. 'I'm sorry about the air-conditioning. We've had brownouts all week.' She smiled agreeably.

'So have we. At least you can open your windows. My office has been like an oven. It's a good thing we decided to meet here,' he said with a smile, glancing around her office, which was an eclectic hodgepodge of paintings by up-and-coming young artists, two important photographs by Avedon that had been a gift to her from the magazine, and layouts from future issues leaning against the walls. There was a mountain of jewelry, accessories, clothes, and fabric samples almost entirely covering the couch, which she unceremoniously dumped on the floor, as her assistant brought in a tray with a pitcher of lemonade and a plate of cookies. Fiona waved John Anderson toward the couch, and handed him a glass of the ice-cold lemonade a moment later, and sat down across from him. 'Thank you. It's nice to finally meet you,' he said politely. She nodded, and looked serious for a moment as she watched him. She hadn't expected him to look quite that uptight, or be that good-looking. He seemed calm and conservative, but at the same time there was something undeniably electric about him, as though there were an invisible current that moved through him. It was so tangible she could feel it. Despite his serious looks, there was something very exciting about him.

She didn't look as he had expected her to either. She was sexier, younger, more striking, and more informal. He had expected her to be older and more of a dragon. She had a fearsome reputation, not for being disagreeable but for being tough, though fair, in her dealings, a force to be reckoned with. And much to his surprise, as she smiled at him over the lemonade, she seemed almost girlish. But despite her seemingly friendly air, within minutes she got to the point of their meeting, and was clear and concise in outlining *Chic*'s expectations. They wanted good solid advertising campaigns, nothing too trendy or exotic. The magazine was the most established in the business, and she expected their advertising to reflect that. She didn't want anything wild or crazy. John was relieved to hear it. *Chic* was a great account for them, and he was beginning to look forward to his dealings with her. More so than before the meeting. In fact, as he drank a second glass of lemonade, and the air-conditioning finally came back on, he had actually decided that he liked her. He liked her style, and the straightforward way she outlined their needs and issues. She had clear, sound ideas about advertising, just as she did about her own business. By the time he stood up to leave, he was almost sorry the meeting was over. He liked talking to her. She was tough and fair. She was totally feminine, and strong at the same time. She was a woman to be feared and admired.

Fiona walked him to the elevator, something she did rarely. She was usually in a hurry to get back to work, but she lingered for a few minutes, talking to him, and she was pleased when she went back to her office. He was a good man, smart, quick, funny, and not as stuffy as he looked in his gray suit, white shirt, and sober navy tie. He looked more like a banker than the head of an ad agency, but she liked the fact that he wore elegant expensive shoes that she correctly suspected he'd bought in London, and his suit was impeccably tailored. He had a definite look about him, in sharp contrast to her own style. In all things, and certainly her taste and style, Fiona was far more daring. She could wear almost anything, and make it look terrific.

She left the office late that afternoon and as always was in a hurry. She hailed a cab outside their offices on Park Avenue, and sped uptown to her brownstone. It was after six when she got home, already wilted from the heat in the cab. And the moment she walked in she could hear chaos in her kitchen. She was expecting guests at seven-thirty. She kept her house ice-cold, as much for her own comfort as for that of her ancient English bulldog. He was fourteen years old, a miraculous age for the breed, and beloved by all who knew him. His name was Sir Winston, after Churchill. He greeted her enthusiastically when she got home, as she hurried into the kitchen to check on progress there, and was pleased to find her caterers working at a frenzied pace, preparing the Indian dinner she had ordered.

Her part-time house man was wearing a loose yellow silk shirt, and red silk harem pants made of sari fabric. He loved exotic clothes, and whenever possible, she brought him wonderful fabrics from her travels. She was always amused by what he turned them into. His name was Jamal, he was Pakistani, and although he was a little fey at times, most of the time he was efficient. What he lacked in expertise in the domestic arts, he made up for in creativity and flexibility, which suited her to perfection. She could spring a dozen people or more on him for dinner at the drop of a hat, he would manage to do fabulous flower arrangements and come up with something for the guests to eat, although tonight the caterers were performing that task for him. There were half a dozen of them in Fiona's kitchen, and Jamal had covered the center of the dining table with moss, delicate flowers, and candles. The whole room had been transformed into an Indian garden, and he had used fuchsia silk place mats and turquoise napkins. The table looked sumptuous. It was just the right look for one of Fiona's parties, which were legendary.

'Perfect!' she approved with a broad smile, and then dashed upstairs to shower and change, with Sir Winston lumbering slowly behind her. By the time the dog got upstairs, Fiona had peeled off her clothes and was in the shower.

21

Forty-five minutes later, she was back downstairs again, in an exquisite lime-green sari. And an hour after that, there were two dozen people in her living room, conversing loudly. They were the usual crop of young photographers, writers her own age, a famous artist and his wife, an ancient editor of *Vogue* who had been Fiona's mentor, a senator, a flock of bankers and businessmen, and several well-known models – a standard evening at Fiona's. Everyone was having a good time, and by the time they reached the dinner table, the conversations had intertwined, people felt like old friends, and Jamal passed trays of champagne and the hors d'oeuvres the caterers had provided. The evening was a success almost before it started. Fiona loved evenings like that, and entertained often. Her dinner parties always appeared casual but in fact were always more carefully orchestrated than she admitted, however impromptu or last minute the arrangements. She was a perfectionist, although she enjoyed eclectic people, and collected an odd assortment of acquaintances from a wide range of artistic fields. And by coincidence more than design, the people at her table were often wonderful to look at. But the star who always stood out among them as the most intriguing, most fashionable, most impressive was Fiona. She had a gift of style and grace and excitement like few others. And she drew interesting people to her like a magnet.

When the last of the guests left at two A.M., she

went up to bed, after thanking Jamal for his efforts. She knew that he would leave the house impeccable, the caterers had left the kitchen immaculate, and Sir Winston was long since snoring in her bedroom. He sounded like a lawn-mower, and it never bothered her, she loved him. She dropped her sari on a chair, slipped into bed in the nightgown Jamal had left out for her, and she was sound asleep five minutes later. And up again the moment the alarm went off at seven. She had a long day ahead of her, they were putting the last of the August issue to bed, and she had a meeting scheduled about the September issue.

She was up to her ears in editors when her secretary buzzed her intercom to tell her John Anderson was on the phone, and she was about to tell her she was too busy and wouldn't take the call, and then thought better of it. It might be important. She had raised a number of questions at their meeting that needed answers, mostly about the budget.

'Good morning,' John said pleasantly. 'Is this a bad time?' he asked innocently, and she laughed. In her life, there was rarely a good one. She was always busy, and usually surrounded by chaos.

'No, it's fine. The usual craziness around here. We're just locking up the August issue, and start-ing on September.'

'Sorry, I didn't mean to interrupt you. I just wanted to tell you how much I enjoyed our meet-ing yesterday.' His voice was deeper than she had remembered it, and it struck her as she listened to him, that he sounded sexy. It wasn't a word she would have used to describe him, but his voice on the phone had a powerfully male timbre to it. He also had the answers to some of her questions, and she liked that. She liked working with people who got the job done quickly. He had obviously put some effort into the research. She made notes of what he said, and he told her he'd fax over more information later. She thanked him, and was about to get off the phone and deal with the chaos around her, when he switched into another gear entirely, and she could almost hear him smiling. The voice evolved suddenly from efficient businessman to something akin to boyish. 'I know this is short notice, Fiona. You sound busy as hell, but do you have time for lunch today? Mine just canceled.' In fact, he was planning to cancel it himself if she would have lunch with him. He'd been thinking about her all morning, and he wanted to see her again. Everything about her intrigued him.

'I . . . actually . . .' She was startled, and thought about it for a minute. They had covered all the ground they needed to the day before, but she told herself it wasn't a bad idea to establish a working relationship with him and get to know him. 'I was going to eat here, today is crazy . . . but . . . can we make it quick? I can probably get out around one-fifteen, and I have to be back here for our September editorial meeting by two-thirty.'

'That'll work. I know a very decent deli near you where we can grab a sandwich. Will that work for you?' He was businesslike and matter-of-fact, and she liked his lack of artifice and pretension. There was a lot she liked about him, and she suspected she was going to like working with him. Far more than she'd expected. He was pleasant and personable, and she might even invite him to a dinner party, when she got back from Paris.

'Sounds great. Where should I meet you?'

'I'll be downstairs at one-ten. Don't worry if you're late,' he said reassuringly. Which was a good thing. She was almost always tardy. She just had too much on her plate, and it was hard to fit it all in. She usually ran twenty to thirty minutes late, like clockwork.

'Perfect. See you then.' She hung up without giving it further thought and went back to her meeting. Adrian was making a presentation to the other editors by then, and it was nearly one-fifteen by the time he finished. She glanced at her watch as the meeting broke up, gathered up her papers, dropped them in her in basket, grabbed her bag, and headed out of her office.

'Where are you off to? Do you want to have lunch?' Adrian asked, smiling at her. The meeting had gone well, and they were both pleased with the look of the August issue now that it was complete.

'Can't. I'm busy. I'm having lunch with our ad agency.' She almost invited Adrian to come, and then didn't.

'I thought you did that yesterday.' He raised an eyebrow. He knew Fiona didn't go out for lunch unless she had to, so it was obviously not social.

'Follow-up.' She wasn't sure if she was lying to him or herself as she headed out. But for some reason, she correctly sensed that her lunch with John Anderson wasn't entirely business. And she didn't mind. He seemed like a nice guy, and a decent person. He was waiting downstairs in a black Lincoln Town Car with a driver. He smiled broadly the moment he saw her. She was wearing pink linen slacks, a white sleeveless shirt, and sandals, and with a straw bag over her shoulder, she looked as if she were going to the beach. It was another day of torrid heat, but it was blissfully cool in the air-conditioned car. And as she got in, she smiled at him.

'You look terrific,' John said admiringly, as she slid in beside him, and they drove off to the deli he had promised. It was only a few blocks, but it was too hot to walk. It was just over a hundred degrees outside. He was wearing a beige suit and a blue shirt, and another serious-looking dark tie. All business, in sharp contrast to Fiona's summer look. She had her hair piled in a loose knot on her head with ivory chopsticks stuck in it. He couldn't resist wondering suddenly what would happen if he pulled them out. He liked the thought of her red hair cascading to her shoulders, as he tried to concentrate on what she was saying.

She was telling him about the meeting she'd just

been in, and he realized as he looked at her that he hadn't heard a word she said. By then, they had reached the deli, and the driver opened the door and helped her out.

The deli was busy and full, looked efficient and clean, and the food smelled delicious. Fiona ordered a salad and iced tea, John ordered a roast beef sandwich and a cup of coffee, and as he looked at her, he found himself randomly wondering how old she was. She was forty-two, but looked ten years younger.

'Is something wrong?' Fiona asked him. He had an odd look on his face, as though he had been struck by something, as the waiter poured his coffee.

'No.' He wanted to tell her he liked her perfume, but was afraid she would think him a fool if he did. She didn't look like the sort of person to mix business with pleasure, and normally neither did he. But there was something vastly unsettling about her, and almost mesmerizing. And he was feeling mesmerized. Without meaning to, she had a seductive quality about her, and he found it hard to keep his mind on business as he sat across the table from her, looking into the deep green eyes that looked back so earnestly at him. She was entirely oblivious to what he was thinking about her. She had never paid much attention to the impact she had on men, she was always too busy thinking and talking about a variety of topics. John was fascinated by her.

'I liked the initial figures you came up with this morning,' she said as their food arrived, and she began picking at her salad. She was so stylishly thin that it was hard to imagine that she ate much, but she didn't look anorexic either. There was just enough meat on her bones to give her figure a look that appealed to him. She looked athletic, and he noticed that she had firm, thin, strong arms. He wondered if she played tennis or swam a lot. The budget for *Chic* magazine was the furthest thing from his mind, as he mused about her.

'What are you doing this summer?' he asked after they had paid cursory homage to the budget. He wanted to know more about her, not just her work. 'Are you going away?'

'I'm going to Paris in two weeks, for the couture shows. And I always go to St. Tropez for a week after that. Afterwards I have to get back here, or I'll be out of a job.' She grinned at him between bites of her salad, and he laughed.

'Somehow I doubt that. Do you go out to the Hamptons on weekends?' He was curious about her life.

'Sometimes. A lot of the time I work through the weekend. Depends what I've got on my plate. I try to take a little time off. And I usually go to the Vineyard on Labor Day. I'll be in France over the Fourth.'

'What are the couture shows like?' He couldn't even imagine them, and they sounded interesting to him. He had never been to a fashion show in his life, let alone one in Paris. But he could easily envision her in that setting, and liked the idea of it. There was something innately exciting and glamorous about her.

'The shows are fun, busy, crazy, beautiful, frenetic. Gorgeous clothes and spectacular models. There are fewer couture houses than there used to be, but it's still a damn good show. Now that you represent the magazine, you should come sometime. You'd love the models, men always do. I can get you tickets if you want. Would your daughters like to go?'

'They might.' He couldn't recall mentioning Hilary and Courtenay to her, but maybe he had. 'Neither of them is passionate about fashion, but a trip to Paris would be hard to resist. We usually go to a ranch in Montana every year. Both of my girls love to ride. I'm not sure we'll make it this year. Both girls have summer jobs. Hilary is going to be working in L.A., and Courtenay took a job at a camp on the Cape. It's a lot harder to take vacations together now that they're in college.' And he hated to admit it, but since their mother died, the family didn't spend as much time together as he liked. They all went separate ways these days, although they spoke frequently, and the ranch in Montana was a bittersweet memory for him. He wasn't unhappy at the prospect of giving up that trip. It reminded him too much of his wife, and the happy summers they had spent there when the girls were little. 'Do you have children, Fiona?' He knew very little about her, other than in the context of her job.

'No, I don't. I've never been married, not that that's a prerequisite these days. Most of the people I know who have children aren't. But no, in answer to your question, I don't have kids.' She didn't look unhappy about it.

'I'm sorry,' he said sympathetically, and she smiled.

'I'm not. I know it sounds awful to admit it, but I've never wanted them. I figure there are lots of people who'd make good parents, and I've never been sure I'd be one of them. I've never wanted to take that chance.' He wanted to say it wasn't too late, but thought it would be presumptuous to tell her that.

'You might surprise yourself. It's hard to warm up to the idea of children till you have your own. I was only lukewarm about it until Hilary was born. It was a lot better than I thought. I'm crazy about my girls. And they're very tolerant of me.' He hesitated for a moment and then went on. 'We've been a lot closer since their mother died, although the girls are busy and have their own lives now. But we speak often, and get together when we can.' They also confided in him more than they used to, now that their mother was gone.

'How long ago was that? Your wife, I mean,' she asked carefully. She wondered if he was still in deep mourning or had adjusted to the loss. He didn't speak of his wife with awe and reverence, but with kindness and warmth, which led her to assume that he had made his peace with her death.

'It'll be two years in August. It seems like a long time sometimes, and only weeks ago at others. She was sick for a long time. Nearly three years. The girls and I had time to adjust, but it's always something of a shock. She was only forty-five when she died.'

'I'm sorry.' She didn't know what else to say, and thinking of it made her sad on his behalf.

'So am I.' He smiled wistfully at her. 'She was a good person. She did everything she could to get us ready to take care of each other before she died. She taught me a lot, about grace under fire. I'm not sure I could have been as strong in her shoes. I'll always admire her for that. She even taught me how to cook.' He laughed at that, and lightened the moment, as Fiona smiled at him. She liked him a lot, far more than she had expected to. Suddenly this had nothing to do with *Chic*, or the new ad agency she'd hired.

'She sounds like a wonderful woman.' Fiona wanted to tell him that she thought he was a wonderful man. The vision of his dying wife teaching him to cook had touched her heart, and she suspected that his girls were nice kids too, if they were anything like him.

'She was terrific. And so are you. I'm enormously impressed by what you do, and the empire you run, Fiona. That's no small task. You must be constantly under pressure, with deadlines every month. I'd have an ulcer in a week.'

'You get used to it. I thrive on it. I think I love the adrenaline rush. I wouldn't know what to do without it. The deadlines keep me on track. You're not running a small empire either.' The agency was the third largest in the world, and he had run an even larger one before that. But moving to the agency he was at now had been a coup for him, it had a golden reputation, and had won a slew of creative awards. It had more prestige than the agency he'd been at previously, even if it was slightly smaller, though not much.

'I love the London office. I wouldn't have minded running it for a few years. Actually, they offered me that first, several years ago, but I couldn't ask Ann to move, she was too sick by then, and I wouldn't have wanted to leave the girls here, they didn't want to leave their schools. In the end, I got a bigger job later by turning them down. And this change came at just the right time. I was ready to move on and do something new. What about you, Fiona? Do you see yourself getting old and gray at *Chic*, or is there something you want to do after this?'

'You don't get old and gray at fashion magazines,' she said with a smile, 'with few exceptions.' Her mentor and predecessor had stayed till she was seventy, but that was rare. 'Most of the time, it's a finite tenure, and I have absolutely no idea what I'd do if I left. At this point, that's not a very appealing thought, and I hope I have a few years left at *Chic*. Maybe even a lot of years, if I'm lucky. But I've always wanted to write a book.'

'Fiction or nonfiction?' he asked with interest. They had finished their lunch by then, but neither of them wanted to leave and go back to work.

'Maybe both. A nonfiction about the fashion world, such as it is. And maybe after that, a novel in the same vein. I loved to write short stories as a kid, and I always wanted to turn them into a book. It would be fun to try, although I'm not sure I could.' It was hard for him to imagine anything she couldn't do, if she set her mind to it. And he could easily envision her writing a book. She was bright and clever and quick, and told some very funny stories about the business. He suspected that she could write something that would be fun to read.

'Do you see yourself doing something after advertising, or instead of?' She was curious about him, just as he was about her. And they were obviously laying the groundwork for some kind of bond that transcended work. Maybe just knowing more about each other, to give depth and character to the contact they were going to have for *Chic*.

'Honestly? No. I've never done anything other than advertising. Maybe golf? I don't know. I'm not sure there's life after work.'

'We all feel that. Most of the time, I just figure I'll die at my desk. Not for a long time, I hope,' she said, feeling awkward, as she remembered his wife's untimely death. 'I don't have time to do much more than work.'

'At least you get to do it in fun places. Paris and St. Tropez don't sound like hardship posts to me.'

'They're not.' She grinned broadly. 'And I've just been invited to spend a few days on a friend's boat when I go to St. Tropez.'

'Now I'm really jealous,' he said, as he paid the check. He knew she had to get back to the office, and he did too.

'Maybe you should come and check it out. Let me know if you want tickets to the shows.'

'When are they?' he inquired with interest. He had never even remotely thought of going to Paris for the couture shows, it would definitely be a first for him if he went. Although it was unlikely he could. He was very busy.

'The last week of June, and first few days of July. They're a lot of fun, particularly if you know people. But even if you don't, they're pretty spectacular to watch.'

'I have a meeting in London on July first. If it looks like I can shake loose for a day or two at either end, I'll let you know.' They were walking back to the car by then, and felt as though they had been sucked up in a vacuum as they hurried from the deli to the car.

'Thank you for lunch, by the way,' she said as she slid in beside him, and five minutes later they were back at her office building, and she turned to

34

smile at him again before she got out. 'This was fun. Thanks, John. I feel like a human being again, going back to work. My staff will thank you for it. Most of the time I skip lunch.'

'We'll have to do something about that, it's not healthy. But I do the same thing,' he confessed with a grin. 'I enjoyed it too. Let's do it again soon,' he said as she got out and smiled at him. And then she hurried into the building as he drove off, thinking about her. Fiona Monaghan was a remarkable woman, beautiful, intelligent, exciting, elegant, and in her own inimitable way, scary as hell. But as he thought about her as he went back to his office, he wasn't scared. John Anderson was seriously intrigued. She was the first woman he'd met in two years who seemed worth more than a second glance. And that she was.

2

The week after she met John Anderson, Fiona
spent two days at an important shoot. Six of the
world's most important supermodels were in it,
four major designers were represented, and the
photographs were shot by Henryk Zeff. He flew in
from London for the shoot, with four assistants,
his nineteen-year-old wife, and their six-month-
old twins. The shoot was fabulous, and Fiona was
sure the photographs would be extraordinary, and
inevitably the entire week turned into a zoo. The
models were difficult and demanding, one of them
used cocaine for most of the shoot, two of
them were lovers and had a humongous fight on
the set, and the most famous and essential of them
was so anorexic, she fainted after eating literally
nothing for the first three days they worked. She
said she was 'fasting,' and the paramedics who
came to revive her suspected that she was suffer-
ing from mono too. They shot some of the
photographs on the beach, wearing fur coats, and
the blazing sun and relentless heat were nearly

enough to kill them all. Fiona stood watching them up to her hips in the water, it was the only relief, as she fanned herself with a huge straw hat. Her cell phone rang late that afternoon, for the ninety-second time. Every other time it had been her office with some new crisis. They were deep into the September issue by then. The shoot they were doing was for October, but this was the only time Zeff had been able to give them, he was solidly booked for the rest of the summer. And this time when the phone rang, it wasn't Fiona's office. It was John Anderson.

'Hi, how are you?' He sounded relaxed and cheerful, despite a long, aggravating day at his end. But he wasn't one to complain, particularly not to someone he didn't know well. He had been fighting all afternoon to keep a major account, which was threatening to walk. He had saved it finally, but felt as though he had spent the entire day giving blood. 'Is this a bad time?' Fiona chuckled at the question.

One of the models had just passed out from the heat, and another one had just thrown a bottle of Evian at Henryk Zeff for taking her out of a shot. 'No, not at all. Perfect time,' Fiona said, laughing. If she'd had a gun, she would have shot them all. 'My models are dropping like flies and having tantrums, one of them just threw something at the photographer, we're all about to keel over from sunstroke and heat prostration, and the photographer's twelve-year-old wife is nursing twins, both of whom have heat rash and haven't stopped crying all week. Just another ordinary day at *Chic*.' He laughed at her description, but to Fiona, it was all too real, even if hard for him to imagine. She was used to this. It was daily fare for her. 'How was your day?'

'It's sounding a lot better now that I've heard yours. I've been running the Paris peace talks here since seven A.M. But I think we won. I just had a crazy idea and thought I'd give you a call. I was wondering if you wanted to have a hamburger with me on your way home.' This time she guffawed.

'I'd love to, except that I'm standing here up to my ass in the Atlantic in two-hundred-degree heat, somewhere on a beach on Long Island, in some godforsaken town with nothing but a bowling alley and a diner, and at this rate, we'll be here till tomorrow morning. Otherwise I'd have loved it. Thanks for asking.'

'We'll do it some other time. What time are you planning to wrap up?'

'After sunset, whenever that is. I think this is supposed to be the longest day of the year. I knew that by about noon, after two of the models slapped each other, and one of them threw up from the heat.'

'I'm glad I don't have your job. Is it always like that?'

'No. Usually, it's worse. Zeff runs a pretty tight ship. He doesn't put up with a lot. He keeps

38

threatening to walk out and expects me to make everyone behave. Good luck on that.'

'Do you always go to the shoots?' He understood little about her job, and had somehow assumed that she sat at a desk, writing about clothes. It was considerably more complicated than that, although she did a lot of writing too, and checking over everyone else's work, for content and style. Fiona ran *Chic* with an iron hand. She worried about the budget and was the most fiscally responsible editor-in-chief they'd ever had. In spite of their vast expenses, the magazine had been in the black for years and turned a handsome profit, in great part thanks to her, and the quality of her product.

'I only go to shoots when I have to. Most of the time, the younger editors take care of that. But if it's dicey enough, or liable to be, I go. This one is. And Zeff is a major star, so are the girls here.'

'Are they modeling bikinis?' he asked innocently, and she laughed even harder.

'No. Fur.'

'Oh, shit.' He couldn't even imagine it in this heat.

'Precisely. We keep having to ice the girls down after they take them off. So far no one has died of the heat, so I guess we're still ahead.'

'I hope you're not wearing fur too,' he teased.

'Nope. I'm standing here in the water, in a bikini. And the photographer's wife has been walking around naked all day, holding her babies.'

'It all sounds very exotic.' Beautiful women wandering around naked or wearing fur on a beach. It was an interesting vision, as he imagined Fiona standing in the ocean in a bikini talking to him on her cell phone. 'Not exactly like my work-day. But I guess it sounds like fun too.'

'Sometimes it is,' she conceded as Henryk Zeff started waving his arms at her in a panic. He wanted to move for their last shot, and all but one of the girls objected, and pleaded exhaustion from the heat. He wanted Fiona to negotiate it for him, which of course she would. 'Looks like I've got to go, the Indians are about to kill the chief. I'm not sure who I feel sorrier for, him or them or me. I'll call you back,' she said, sounding distracted. 'Probably tomorrow.' It was already seven-fifteen, she realized, as she glanced at her watch, and she was surprised he was still in the office.

'I'll call you,' he said calmly, but she was already gone, as he sat pensively at his desk. Her life seemed light-years from his, although the art department in the agency was certainly not un-familiar with a life like hers. But John rarely dealt with them and never went on shoots. He was far too busy soliciting new accounts, and keeping the existing ones happy, and overseeing vast amounts of money being spent on ad campaigns. The details of how those campaigns were put together were someone else's problem and not his. But he was undeniably intrigued by Fiona's world. It sounded fascinating and exotic to him, although

40

Fiona would have disagreed with him, as she helped the assistants pack Henryk's equipment, while his wife had a tantrum, and he argued with her, and both babies cried. The models were languishing under umbrellas, drinking warm lemonade from a huge container, and threatening to quit, trying to negotiate hardship pay, and calling their agencies on their cell phones. They said no one had told them how long the shoot would be, or that it would involve fur. One of the models had already threatened to walk out on principle, and said she was going to report them to PETA, who would surely demonstrate in front of the magazine, as they had before, if they featured fur too prominently.

It was another hour before they were fully set up in the new location half a mile down the beach, and it was nearly sunset by then. They had just enough time for the last shot, and Henryk was busily shouting everyone into place. By then, his wife was asleep in the car with the twins. And Fiona realized she was exhausted as she watched the last of the shoot. It was after nine before they got everyone dressed and off the beach, all the camera equipment packed up, and the models into the limousines that *Chic* had hired for the day. The catering truck was already gone. Henryk and his wife and babies took off first. And Fiona was the last to leave. She had rented a Town Car for herself, and closed her eyes and put her head back against the seat as they drove away. It was nearly eleven when she got home. But from a technical standpoint, it had been a perfect day. She knew the shots would be great, and none of the problems would ever show.

But as she climbed the stairs to her bedroom, she felt a hundred years old. And she smiled when she found Sir Winston snoring loudly on her bed. She envied him the life he led. She was too tired to eat dinner, or even go downstairs to the kitchen for something to drink. She had an acute case of heartburn after drinking lemonade all day. And when her cell phone rang, she stared at it for a long moment, too tired to reach out and fish it out of her bag. She knew in another two rings it would go to voice mail, and she didn't care. And then at the last second, she realized it might be Henryk, with some dire problem after the shoot. Maybe they had an accident on the way back and lost all the film, or got kidnapped by a UFO.

'Yes?' she said in a flat, nearly unrecognizable voice. She was almost too tired to care.

'God, you sound dead. Are you okay?' It was John, and she didn't recognize his voice.

'I *am* dead. Who is this, and why are you calling me?' At least it wasn't Henryk. The voice was American, not British, and no one normally cared if she was dead or not. Not in a long time anyway.

'It's John. I'm sorry, Fiona, were you asleep?'

'Oh. Sorry. I was afraid it was something to do with the shoot. I was afraid they lost the film. I just got home.'

'You work too hard,' he said sympathetically. He genuinely felt sorry for her. She sounded as beat as she felt.

'I know. That's what they pay me for, I guess. How are you?' she asked as she stretched out on the bed, and closed her eyes. Sir Winston opened one eye, saw her lying there, rolled over on his back, and snored louder. She smiled at the familiar noise, he sounded like a 747 landing on her roof, and John heard it too.

'What's that noise?' She sounded like she had an electric power saw in her arms, which was close.

'Sir Winston.'

'Who's that?' John sounded startled.

'Don't tell him I called him that, but he's my dog.'

'Your dog sounds like that? My God, what is he, or what's wrong with him? He sounds like *The Texas Chainsaw Massacre* in THX.'

'It's part of his charm. He's an English bull. When I lived in an apartment, my downstairs neighbors kept complaining, they could hear him through my floor. They thought I was running heavy machinery, they refused to believe it was a dog till I invited them up one night when he was asleep.'

'You don't sleep with him, do you?' It was obvious to him she didn't. How could she with all that racket?

'Of course I do. He's my best friend. We've been together for fourteen years, he's the longest relationship I've ever had, and the best one,' she said proudly.

'Now there's a subject to explore sometime when you're not so tired. I actually called to see how you were after the shoot, and to see if you want to have dinner tomorrow night.' He was determined to see her again before she left for Paris, and she was constantly on his mind. She had been since he met her.

'What day is tomorrow?' she asked, opening her eyes. Her mind was blank. She was truly dead tired.

'The twenty-second. I know it's short notice, I've had a crazy week, and I had a client dinner I was ecstatic they canceled.' He spent most of his nights entertaining clients, and he was always thrilled to have a night to himself.

'Damn,' she suddenly remembered, 'I can't. I'm sorry,' and then she decided to include him in her plans. He would be a bit of an odd man in the group, but she enjoyed that, as long as he didn't mind. 'I'm having people in to dinner, it's always very informal here. And pretty last minute. I just organized it last week. I have some musician friends coming in from Prague, and a bunch of artists I haven't seen in ages. One of my editors from the magazine is coming, and I can't remember who else. I'm just doing pasta and a salad.'

'Don't tell me you cook too.' He sounded genuinely impressed, and she laughed.

'Not if I can help it. I have someone come in to

do it.' This time Jamal and not the caterers was doing the dinner. She had told everyone that if the heat wasn't too unbearable, they would eat in her garden. On warm summer nights, that was relaxing and nice. And Jamal made fabulous pasta. He had wanted to do paella, but she didn't trust the shellfish in the heat, which seemed wise, so she had told him to make pasta. With enough wine on hand, no one seemed to care much about the food. 'Would you like to come? Just wear jeans and a shirt, you don't have to wear a tie.' She couldn't imagine him without one.

'It sounds like fun. Do you entertain often?'

'When I have time. And sometimes even when I don't. I like seeing friends, and there always seems to be someone coming through town. Do you entertain, John?' She didn't have a sense yet for what his private life was like, only that he liked to travel with his children. He hadn't said much yet about the rest.

'Only for business, in restaurants. But it's more an obligation than a pleasure. I haven't given a dinner party since my wife died. She used to love entertaining.' She had that in common with Fiona, although their styles were vastly different. Ann Anderson had given proper little dinner parties for their friends in Greenwich. They had only moved into the city after she got sick, because it was easier for her to be close to the hospital for treatment. And she had been too sick by then to entertain. She had spent her last two years in their

45

current apartment, which made it a sad place for him now, but he didn't say that to Fiona. 'It's hard entertaining when you're single,' he said plaintively, and then felt foolish. She was single, and always had been, and it didn't seem to stop her. Nothing stopped Fiona from doing what she wanted. He liked that about her.

'You just have to be more casual about it. People don't expect as much from single people socially, so whatever you do for them seems terrific. Sometimes, the less you do, the more they like it.' Fiona did more than she admitted, but she made it look effortless and spontaneous, which was part of the magic she created when she entertained. 'So will you come for dinner tomorrow?' She hoped he would, although the group she had invited was more eclectic than usual, and she wondered if he'd find them strange or too exotic.

'I'd love to. What time do you want me?' He sounded enthused.

'Eight o'clock. I'll be in meetings until seven. I'm going to have to run like hell to be here before the guests.' That wasn't unusual in her life either.

'Can I bring anything?' he offered, trying to be helpful, although he suspected she had everything arranged. Fiona was not someone to leave even the remotest detail to chance. She hadn't gotten where she was by being casual or vague.

'Just bring yourself. See you tomorrow night then.'

'Good night,' he said gently, and they hung up.

She put on her nightgown after that, and brushed her teeth, thinking of him. She liked him, and felt an undeniable attraction to him, although he was entirely different from any other man who had appealed to her. She had gone out with a few conservative preppy guys when she was young. But in recent years, she had been drawn to artistic, creative men, which had always ended up in disaster. Maybe it was time for a change. She was still thinking about him when she slipped into bed next to Sir Winston, who rolled over with a groan and went on snoring more loudly than ever. It was a familiar sound that always lulled her to sleep. And as always, she slept straight through until her alarm went off at seven.

She put Sir Winston in the garden for a few minutes, took a shower, read the paper, had coffee, dressed, and left for work. And it was another endless day at *Chic*. She spent most of the day with Adrian, solving problems and going through photographs of several shoots they'd done the previous week. She couldn't wait to see the ones taken by Henryk Zeff. She already knew that they'd be great. Adrian was coming to dinner that night, and she didn't tell him John Anderson would be there. She knew that if she did, he'd make a comment, and wonder why she had invited him. She wasn't sure why herself. She still needed time to figure it out. And she didn't want to make a big deal of it. It might turn out to be one of those mild mutual attractions that went nowhere. Or more than likely, they'd just be friends, if that. They were so immensely different, the likelihood of anything coming of it seemed slim to none to her. They'd probably drive each other insane. They were better off as friends. She was still telling herself that when she went home that night, and found Jamal tossing a huge salad in the kitchen and making garlic bread. He had also made canapés. She tasted one of them when she came in. He was wearing hot pink capri pants, gold Indian sandals, and was bare-chested. Most of her friends were used to Jamal's exotic getups, and she thought they lent her evenings a festive air, although she wondered about his not wearing a shirt, and she mentioned it to him.

'Do you think it's a little too casual?' she asked, as she tried another of the hors d'oeuvres. They were great.

'It's too hot to wear anything,' he said, sticking the bread in the oven. She noticed on the kitchen clock that she had forty minutes to get dressed.

'Well, stick with the pants, Jamal. It's a good look.' He had worn a gold jewel-encrusted loincloth once, which even she had admitted was a bit much, or actually not quite enough in that case. 'I love the sandals, by the way. Where'd you get them?' She had seen a pair like that once, but couldn't remember where.

'They're yours. I found them in the back of the closet. You never wear them. I thought I'd borrow them for tonight. Do you mind?' He looked artless

48

and innocent as he asked, and she stared at them and laughed.

'I thought they looked familiar. Now that I think about it, I think they hurt. Keep them if you like them. They look better on you.' They had been Blahnik samples specially made for a shoot several years ago.

'Thank you,' he said sweetly, as he tested the salad dressing on a lettuce leaf, and she hurried upstairs.

Half an hour later, she was back downstairs wearing white silk pants and a gossamer-thin gold shirt, with huge hoop diamond earrings, high-heeled gold sandals, and her hair hanging down her back in a thick braid. She and Jamal looked almost like a matched set. He had put plates, napkins, and cutlery on the table in the garden, and there were candles and flowers everywhere. She tossed some big cozy cushions around in case people wanted to sit on the floor, and put some music on, just as the first guests came through the door. She had almost forgotten who she'd asked, and had glanced at a list upstairs. It was the usual unusual assortment, artists, writers, photographers, models, lawyers, doctors, the musicians who had come from Prague. There were a couple of Brazilians she'd met recently, two Italians, and a woman one of them brought who spoke French, and by sheer coincidence one of the musicians discovered that the woman also spoke Czech. She said her father had been French and her mother

Czech. It was the perfect blend, and as Fiona looked around at the nearly two dozen people in her garden, she suddenly saw John wander through her living room in immaculate pressed jeans and a starched white shirt. He was wearing Hermès loafers without socks. He looked every bit as impeccable as he did in a suit, and he didn't have a hair out of place. And despite the lack of imagination he showed in his wardrobe, she liked his look. He looked manly and elegant, immaculate, and perfectly put together, and she found all of it remarkably attractive. And when he kissed her cheek, she liked the cologne he wore as well. And he commented on hers. It was the same scent she had worn for twenty years. She had it made for her in Paris, and it was a signature for her. Everyone who knew her recognized it, and people always commented on it. It was just warm enough and cool enough, with a slightly spicy scent. And she loved the fact that it was hers alone, and had no name. Adrian called it Fiona One, and she'd had cologne made for him as well. He was there that night too, and he was watching her when John walked in. She introduced them to each other, as Jamal offered John champagne. Fiona told him that Adrian was the most important editor at *Chic*.

'She flatters me instead of giving me a raise,' Adrian teased, taking John in. And like Fiona, he liked what he saw, he liked his style and self-confidence and quiet grace, and he could see that she liked it, too. She was standing close to John as the others milled around, and she introduced him to everyone in the group.

'This is quite a collection of people,' he said quietly in a moment's lull, after Adrian moved away to talk to one of the Czechs.

'It's a little weirder than usual, but it seemed like fun. I do more serious dinners in winter. In summer, it's fun to be a little crazier.' He nodded and seemed to agree, although he had never been to a dinner quite like this. Her house looked beautiful, and warm and welcoming, and there seemed to be a million tiny treasures everywhere, mostly things she had found on trips and brought home with her. He seemed to be looking for something, and then turned to her.

'Where's the power saw?'

'What power saw?'

'The guy snoring in your bed last night.'

'Sir Winston? He's upstairs. He hates guests. He thinks this is his house. Would you like to meet him?' She was pleased that he'd asked. It was a definite point for him.

'Will he object?' He looked mildly concerned.

'He'll be honored.' It was a good excuse to show John the rest of the house. The living room, dining room, and kitchen were on the main floor, and there was a cozy library on the second floor, and a guest room next to it. The colors she had chosen were all warm caramel and chocolate, with accents of white and a little red to spice it up.

She seemed to favor suedes, silks, and fur. She had exquisite beige silk drapes trimmed in red. Her bedroom and dressing room were on the top floor, with a tiny office she used when she worked at home, which was rare. It was the perfect house for her. There had been a second bedroom on the top floor, which she had turned into a closet when she moved in.

When John was halfway up the stairs, he heard the loud snoring. And as they walked into her bedroom, which was all done in beige silk, even the walls, John saw him on the bed. Sir Winston was sleeping and never stirred. Fiona gently patted him, and he finally picked up his head with considerable effort and a groan and stared at them, and a moment later, he dropped his head back on the bed again with a sigh, and closed his eyes. He made no attempt to introduce himself to John. He seemed entirely indifferent to him, as John grinned.

'He looks like a very proper old gentleman. He doesn't seem to be worried about a strange man in your room,' John commented with amusement. He really was a funny old dog, and he started snoring loudly again as they stood there. He had his head on her pillow, and a favorite toy next to him.

'He knows he's the master of the house. He has nothing to worry about, and he knows it. This is his kingdom, and I'm his slave.'

'Lucky guy.' John smiled at her and glanced

around the room. There were a few silver-framed photographs of Fiona with assorted celebrities and political figures, a few famous actors, two presidents, and one she pointed out to John as a particular favorite, of herself and Jackie Kennedy when she first started at *Chic*. And in spite of the simple decor, there was something elegant and feminine about her room. There was a subtle but unmistakable style to it, and it was instantly obvious that no man lived there. She had never shared the house with anyone except Sir Winston. 'I like your house, Fiona. It's cozy and comfortable and elegant, informal and yet stylish, just like you. I can see you everywhere.'

'I love it,' she said as they left her bedroom, and went back downstairs to the guests. Her tiny office had red lacquer walls and Louis XV chairs upholstered in real zebra skins. And there was a handsome zebra rug on the floor. And a small portrait of her by a famous artist on the wall. There was nothing male about a single corner of the house. As they got back downstairs, Adrian stood watching them, and smiled. He was wearing a white T-shirt and white jeans, and red alligator sandals Manolo Blahnik had made for him in a size fourteen.

'Did she give you a tour?' Adrian asked with interest.

'I introduced him to Sir Winston,' Fiona explained, as Jamal announced dinner with a little Tibetan gong that had a pretty sound and reminded everyone to eat. Everything about Fiona and her surroundings was exotic, from her half-naked Pakistani house man to her friends, and in some ways even her house and dog, although they were slightly more traditional, but not much. There was very little traditional about her, or predictable, and she liked it that way. But so did John. He had come to realize in a matter of days that she was the most exciting woman he had ever met in his life. He thought she had more style than he had ever seen wrapped up in one human being. And Adrian would have agreed with him, most people did.

'What did he think?' Adrian asked seriously, as John listened to their exchange with amusement. He liked her editor friend as well. He looked a little eccentric and creative, but he could tell from speaking to him that Adrian was an exceptionally intelligent and interesting man, despite his slightly flamboyant taste in shoes.

'He thought he was adorable, of course,' Fiona filled in for him, with a smile at John.

'Not John. Of course he thought Sir Winston was adorable. He's not going to tell you he thinks he's a spoiled, smelly old dog, no matter what he really thinks. I meant, what did Sir Winston think? Did he approve?'

'I don't think he was impressed,' John chimed in with a grin. 'He slept through the entire interview. Very loudly!'

'That's a good sign,' Adrian said with a smile at

both of them, and then moved away toward the food. There were four different kinds of pasta in gigantic terracotta bowls, three kinds of salad, and the garlic bread smelled fabulous. There was hardly any of the pungent bread left by the time Fiona and John got to the table Jamal had set up in the garden, and the gardenias Jamal had decorated the table with sent off a heady romantic scent, as John picked up one of them and tucked it into her braid.

'Thank you for inviting me. I love being here.' He felt as though he had entered a magic world that night, and he had. Fiona's world. He saw her as the magic princess at the center of it, weaving her spell on them all. He could feel the essence of her seeping into his pores, at the same time weakening him and giving him strength. His head was nearly spinning at the excitement of her, and in spite of herself, she was beginning to feel the same way about him. She didn't really want to, but she was beginning to feel an irresistible pull toward him. They shared a small iron bench as they ate dinner, and chatted quietly, as Adrian watched with interest from the living room. He knew her well, and could see that Fiona was definitely smitten, but so was John. He looked totally bowled over by her, but who wouldn't be, Adrian commented to a photographer who had noticed it too, and said they made a handsome though unlikely pair. They both knew that Fiona hadn't been involved with anyone in nearly two years, and if this was what she wanted, they were glad for her. She hadn't said anything to Adrian yet, but he knew she would before long, if there was anything to it. He had a feeling they were going to be seeing a lot of John Anderson, and he hoped so for Fiona's sake, if that was what and whom she wanted, for however long. They both knew that forever after wasn't in her plans. But a year or two would suit her fine.

Adrian always thought it was unfortunate that she was alone, although she claimed that she preferred it that way. He never quite believed her, and suspected she was lonely at times, which explained her excessive attachment to her ridiculous old dog. In truth, when she came home at night, Fiona had no one else. Except Jamal. She gave great parties and had interesting friends, some of whom were devoted to her. But she had no one to share her life with, and Adrian always thought it was a waste of a great woman that she had never found a man who was right for her. He found himself hoping, in a melancholy sentimental way, that John would turn out to be the one for her.

John was one of the last guests to leave, but he didn't think it appropriate to be the very last one. It was nearly one in the morning when he thanked her for the evening, and kissed her cheek.

'I had a wonderful time, Fiona. Thank you for inviting me. Please pay my respects to Sir Winston. I'd go upstairs, but I don't want to disturb him. Tell him I send my best and thank him for his hospitality,' he said, as he held her hand lightly on the way out, and she smiled at him. She had a tender spot for him because he understood how important the dog was to her. Most people thought he was a silly old beast, as Adrian did, but he meant the world to her. Sir Winston was all she had in a sentimental sense, and because of that he was even more precious to her.

'I'll be sure to tell him,' Fiona said solemnly, and John kissed her lightly on the cheek again as he left. He could smell the gardenia that he had put in her hair this time. It had a breathtaking effect mixed with her perfume, but everything about Fiona seemed breathtaking to him, and he hated to leave. It was like leaving Brigadoon, and he wondered if he'd ever see her again once he crossed the bridge back to the real world. The only world that seemed real to him now was hers, and it was the only one he wanted.

'I'll call you tomorrow,' he whispered, so no one else would hear. She nodded and smiled and went back to her other guests, still smiling at the thought of him. But she was still of two minds about him, both attracted to him and afraid at the same time. And in the end, as always, Adrian was the last to leave, and he couldn't resist teasing her about John.

'You're falling hard, Miss Monaghan. Like a ton of bricks, I'd say. But for once, I approve. He's respectable, intelligent, responsible, employed, nice, good-looking, and head over heels in love with you, or he will be soon. He's well on his way.' But Adrian was pleased for her, and he approved wholeheartedly.

'No, he's not. We don't even know each other. We just met last week.' She tried to sound more sensible than she was feeling. But she didn't want Adrian to know how much she liked John. Who knew where it would go? Probably nowhere, she told herself, trying to remain cool about it.

'Since when do those things take a long time to happen? The right ones never do. The right man walks into your life, and you know it instantly, Fiona. It's the wrong ones that take a long time to figure out. The good guys knock you right off your feet and on your ass. Or is it the other way around? Anyway, I have a good feeling about this man, Fiona. Now don't go running scared and tell him you want to be alone. At least give the guy a chance.'

'We'll see,' Fiona said mysteriously, as Jamal snuffed all the candles out, and picked up plates and glasses from the tables in the garden. The evening had been a big success, as usual. But more so than ever for her. It had been surprisingly nice, and even comfortable, to have John with her. And he had seemed unexpectedly expansive with her wide variety of guests. He was friendly and at ease with everyone.

'You can't live in this house with a man, you know,' Adrian volunteered sensibly. 'It's too you. He'll never feel comfortable here, if he moves in.'

58

'I didn't invite him to. And I'm never going to live anywhere else. This is my home. Besides, isn't that a little premature?' She pretended to scowl at Adrian, and then laughed at him. 'Sir Winston and I are perfectly happy here on our own.'

'Bullshit. You get as lonely as everyone else. We all do. You may be perfect, Fiona Monaghan, but you're human too. It would do you good to live with a man. I vote for John. He looks like a keeper to me.' It frightened her, and she didn't admit it to Adrian, but she thought so too.

'Sir Winston would never tolerate it. He would consider it an infidelity to him. Besides, I couldn't give up the closet space. I've never met a man who was worth giving up a closet for,' she said stubbornly, but they both knew that wasn't true. She had been very much in love with the conductor who had finally left her for someone else because she refused to marry him. And with the architect who wanted to leave his wife for her. The trouble with Fiona was that she was terrified of marriage and in some ways of getting too attached to men. She didn't want them to abandon her, and she knew that eventually they all would. Or at least that was her worst fear. Just knowing her father had abandoned her, and after the evil step-fathers she'd seen come and go, Fiona had made a decision years ago never to fully trust any man. And Adrian knew that if she didn't break down her walls one day, she would in fact wind up alone. It seemed a reasonable fate to her, but not

59

to him. She accepted it as her destiny, embraced it in fact, and insisted that she was happiest alone.

'Don't be foolish,' Adrian warned her as he left. Jamal was gone by then. 'Compromise a little this time, Fiona. Give this guy a chance.'

'I'm too old to compromise,' she said, perhaps honestly, but in any case, it was what she believed.

'Then sell this house and move in with him, or buy a house together. But don't give up a good man for a brownstone, a career, and a dog.'

'People have given men up for worse things, Adrian,' she said solemnly. 'Besides, I haven't even had a date with him. And maybe I never will.'

'You will,' Adrian said quietly, concerned about her. 'I promise you that. You will. And this one is a good man.' He hoped she wouldn't miss the boat this time. She always did. Always saw to it that she did. And all Adrian could hope, as he got into a cab and sped uptown, was that this time the dog would lose, and the man would win. And for what it was worth, he was putting his money on John.

3

John called her the morning after her dinner party, and thanked her again for including him. But she had only a few minutes to spend with him on the phone. She was swamped. She was leaving for the Hamptons that afternoon, to stay with friends, and going to Paris the following week. She said she had a million things to do, and when he asked her to dinner, she said she didn't have time to see him before she left, which was relatively true. She could have changed some plans for him, but she didn't think that was a smart move. She was trying her best to resist her overwhelming attraction to him. She didn't want things to move faster than was comfortable for her, and she still wasn't sure she wanted to succumb to the lure of him. Emotional involvements were always dangerous, and she was leery of them. And if anything was going to happen, she wanted it to go slow, to give her time to think. She was in no hurry to rush into anything with him, no matter how appealing he was. And there was no denying he was very appealing. Maybe even too much so. She was suspicious of her own feelings for him. They were so powerful and nearly irresistible, it made her want to run away.

'In that case, you leave me no choice,' he said sensibly.

'About what?' She sounded confused. He had that effect on her, and it made her feel out of control, which frightened her.

'About seeing you. I guess I'll take you up on your offer, for a ticket to one of the fashion shows. I have meetings in London on the first, and I could fly to Paris late that afternoon. Is there a show I could come to then? But only if it's not a nuisance for you.' He didn't want to be a pest, but he wanted to see her again. And Paris appealed to him a great deal. She was startled by his offer.

'Are you serious?' She sounded stunned.

'I am. How does that fit into your plans?'

'Actually, that might be fun for you.' She tried to sound like a docent at an art exhibit rather than a woman he was pursuing, just for her own peace of mind. If she thought about it too much otherwise, she knew she'd get too scared. This was almost threatening. She was much too attracted to him. But on the other hand, he seemed like an incredibly nice man. He had no obvious defects, no visible character flaws, no bad reputation from all she'd heard. He was a good man. And she knew only too well how rare that was. So for the moment at least, she wasn't running scared. But she wasn't offering him closet space either, as Adrian had suggested she should. All she was going to do, if he was serious about coming to Paris, was offer to book a room for him at the Ritz. He would have plenty of closets of his own. 'The Dior show is the night of the first, and it's the most theatrical and spectacular. I think you'll enjoy it, although the clothes aren't easy for anyone to wear. But Galliano does the show in unusual locations, and the clothes are incredible. If you like it, we can go to Lacroix the next day, which is always beautiful and almost like living sculpture. I'll get you a seat for both. And there's a big party the night of Dior. Would you like to come to that?'

'I'd love to come to anything you want me at. I don't want to intrude on you, Fiona. I know you have to work. I don't want to get in your way, but I'd love to come to any and all of it. I'm taking a few days off over the Fourth, and I don't have to rush back. My girls are both busy this year, so I can hang around as long as you want. Or leave the day after the Dior show, if you prefer.'

'Why don't we play it by ear? See how much you enjoy it, you might hate it. But most of the time it's a lot of fun. And if you've never seen the couture shows, they're a real spectacle, and the parties are fabulous. Everyone goes all out for the haute couture. It's like an art form in France, even cabdrivers know about it, and talk about the shows as though they've seen them. They're very proud of all that in Paris. I think it's terrific of you to come over. Do you want me to get you a room at the hotel? We all stay at the Ritz. They may be booked, but I can give them a call, they know me pretty well.'

'That would be wonderful, Fiona. Just tell me where to show up when.' He was pleased with himself, and even more so with her. It was fun to step outside the confines of his safe, familiar world. And into her far more exotic one. It promised to be a real adventure for him. And maybe even for her too. Although Fiona seemed to vacillate between being warm and impersonal with him, which was a manifestation of her own ambivalence toward him.

'I'll have my secretary send you an itinerary.' She made it sound as though they were just friends, which worried him. She had been a lot friendlier the night before, but she had awakened worrying that she might have been too friendly – particularly if Adrian was talking about sharing closets. She wondered if she had given John the wrong impression at her dinner party. She didn't want him to think that she was chasing him, or too available. They both needed time to think about what they were doing before they did it, no matter how tempting it was. That was all the more reason to move cautiously, and she had every intention of doing that, particularly if he was coming to Paris. But she was thrilled he had decided to come. It was going to be a lot of fun to have him there, and she said as much to him. He could hardly wait. And she called him back an hour later to tell him he had a room at the hotel, near hers. There were only a few left, and she was relieved to have snagged one of them for him. She always stayed in the same suite on the Cambon side of the hotel. There were no rooms left overlooking the Place Vendôme, and she suspected he would have liked one of them, but she had to take what she could get, and had on his behalf.

'Thanks a million, Fiona, that'll be great.' He made a note to have his secretary call the hotel, give them his credit card details, and arrange to have a car pick him up at Charles de Gaulle. He was thrilled to know it was less than a week away. And Fiona was equally so as she drove to East Hampton late that afternoon. She was mildly sorry she had decided not to see him before she left. It might have been easier than seeing him again in Paris, for the first time since her dinner party. It felt a little weird that they hadn't had a date yet, and he was meeting her in Paris, but they would have plenty to keep them occupied. And Adrian would be there. She could send them off together, if Adrian was free and she had to work. But she was going to try and spend as much free time with John as she could. It was a great way to get to know each other, and a great place to do it.

She nearly had an accident thinking about him, in the heavy traffic on the Sunrise Highway, and she didn't get to East Hampton till that night. The traffic had been horrendous, and she was happy to see her friends. It was an easy, relaxed weekend with one of the senior editors of the magazine, her husband, and her kids. And when Fiona got home on Sunday night, John called.

'How's my rival?'

'Who would that be?' She sounded happy and relaxed after her weekend on the beach. And she was feeling more comfortable about him, particularly since she hadn't seen him all weekend.

'Sir Winston, of course. Did you take him to East Hampton?'

'He hates the beach. It's too hot for him, and he can't swim. He spent the weekend with Jamal. He just brought him home. He's always mad at me when I go away. He's going to summer camp next week.' In this case, it was truly a dog's life, one any man would have envied him, and John nearly did. He particularly liked the thought of lying around, sleeping on her bed, minus the snores.

'He's a lucky guy,' John said cryptically, and they discussed last details of the trip to Paris, and what sort of clothes he should bring. She told him then that nothing planned was black tie, but he needed a couple of dark suits. The Dior party was usually dressy. And there might be one given by Givenchy. *Chic* always gave a cocktail party, as did most of the big designers. Valentino, Versace, Gaultier, and Chanel always gave one in Coco Chanel's apartment on the rue Cambon. They weren't going to lack for entertainment and social life. And the party *Chic* gave at the Ritz was always fun. Adrian was in charge of organizing it and inviting the guests. He always invited every movie star, singer, designer, celebrity socialite, and royal he could lay his hands on. People begged to come.

She made a mental note the next day to tell Adrian to include John in the party *Chic* gave. John sounded genuinely excited about the trip. And in spite of her occasional conflict and concern about him, she still found John hard to resist, and she was just as excited as he. It was going to be fun to have someone to share Paris with. Someone other than Adrian and her other editors. It was going to be nice to be with a man again, for whatever reason, whatever purpose, friendship or other, for however long. And as she hurried off to a meeting thinking about it, she decided in a moment of bravado to give it a fair chance with John and throw caution to the winds. Who could tell, he might just be worth it. And what would life be without excitement and romance?

4

The night flight to Charles de Gaulle from JFK was always too brief. Fiona did some work, ate dinner, settled back in the reclining seat under the comforter Air France provided in first class, slept for a few hours – and then hit the ground running.

She was at the Ritz by ten A.M., and after a shower, a change of clothes, and a cup of coffee, Fiona had a million things to do. She had meetings with the press attachés of the couture houses, usually met with the designer himself, and always got a glimpse of a few of the choice items from the show, which was a sign of their deep respect for her. Few editors, however important, were allowed into the inner sanctums of the couture houses and workrooms, the *ateliers*, before the shows. Fiona was. And after making the rounds of the most important houses on the first day, she met with Adrian and both their assistants that afternoon. Jet lag hadn't even had time to hit her by then, and Adrian was up to his ears in last-minute arrangements for the party they were giving. Fiona had already told him to put John on the list.

She and Adrian had dinner at Le Vaudeville that night, which was a small bistro they both liked, near the stock exchange, and where they were less likely to meet fashion people. Otherwise, they both liked L'Avenue, but Fiona wasn't in the mood to meet a dozen other editors, or a million models, who hung out there and at Costes as well. Her favorite restaurant of course had always been Le Voltaire, on the Left Bank on the Quai Voltaire. But they were both tired on their first evening, and happy to share a huge platter of oysters, and a salad, and go back to the hotel. They both knew that by the next day everyone would be in high gear and moving at full speed. The first show would be that night, and John was arriving from London in the late afternoon. Adrian had already teased her about it, and she had brushed him off, they had plenty of other things to talk about. The clothes they were going to be seeing, some of which Fiona had previewed that day, were for the winter season, and they were going to be fabulous if the samples she'd seen were any indication. The wedding dress at Chanel was beyond belief, with a heavy white velvet bell-shaped skirt bordered in white ermine, and a matching ermine cape trailing behind it, and it looked as if there were shimmering snowflakes resting on the veil. It was magical.

When she and Adrian said good night, she closed her door, took off her clothes, and was in bed in less than ten minutes. And she didn't hear another sound until her wake-up call the next day. It was a glorious, sunny summer day in Paris, and the sunlight was streaming into her room. She always slept with her curtains open in Paris, because she loved the light and the sky, night or day. There was a luminous glow to the night sky that fascinated her, almost like a large black pearl. She loved lying in bed and looking at it until she fell asleep.

Fiona's second day in Paris was even busier than the day before, and John had already arrived by the time she got back to the hotel late that afternoon. He called her room almost as soon as she came through the door.

'You must be psychic,' she teased. 'I just walked in.'

'I know,' he confessed. 'The concierge told me. I was talking to him about restaurant reservations. Where would you like to go?'

'I always love Le Voltaire.' It was small and chic and cozy, and all of the most elegant people in Paris went there, crowded at little tables, or squeezed into the two tiny booths. There was barely space enough for thirty people in the entire room, but it was where everyone who was anyone wanted to go. 'But we're going to the Dior party tonight anyway, and I think Givenchy is doing something tomorrow. We can go to the Versace cocktail party before or after. Maybe we can go to the Voltaire after our party, if you're still here.' She wasn't entirely sure how long he was staying or how much high fashion he could stand. Most men would have had their fill, and then some, after a day or two, and he didn't look the type to linger long in a woman's world. She could never get enough of it, and it was her business. John was just a tourist.

'I'm here for the duration, if you want me,' he announced gamely, which was news to her. Originally, they had discussed a day or two. 'I don't want to be a nuisance, or get in your way. I don't have to go back to London. We wrapped it all up today, and I cleared the decks in New York. So you've got me if you want me, and if you don't, then just ship me off and I'll go home.' He sounded more philosophical than he felt. He had sensed her conflict and ambivalence about pursuing their attraction to each other and didn't want to scare her.

'Why don't you see how you feel about it after you get a taste of it?' she said vaguely. 'You may be sick to death of haute couture in a day or two.' But he knew it would take longer than that to be sick of her, at least he hoped so, but he didn't say that to her.

'So what are our plans? When do you want me?'

'The Dior show is at seven. That's what the invitation says. If we're lucky, they'll start at nine. Dior is always a zoo, they never start on schedule, they're always late. They'll still be sewing beads on dresses and finishing hems at seven, but it's the

71

best show. And they do it in crazy locations they announce at the last minute. We just found out it's at the train station, so it's not too far away. If we leave here at seven-thirty, we'll be fine. I don't want to sit there for two hours. And if by some miracle they start earlier than usual, we'll still be okay.'

'Coat and tie, I assume?' He had no point of reference, and Fiona laughed at the question.

'You can go naked if you want. At Dior, no one will notice.'

'I'm not sure if that's reassuring or insulting.' At least he hoped she would, but she had given him no indication that she was going to pursue, or even accept, a romantic liaison with him, particularly a physical one. He had sensed the magnetic pull between them from the beginning, but there were times when she was very cool. And despite the romantic surroundings in the most beautiful city in the world, here Fiona appeared to be all business. But that was, after all, why she was here, so he understood it. He wondered if they'd get any time alone before he left. But whether or not they did, he knew he would enjoy being with her, and it was fun for him to be immersed in a world that was so entirely different. This was a rare treat for him, and he was excited to share it with her. He suspected it would give him huge insights into her and the world she ate, slept, drank, and breathed. Fashion was the very fiber of her being.

'I'll meet you downstairs at seven-fifteen,' she said briskly. She had calls to return and things to do before she met up with him, and then suddenly her voice softened, and she sounded more human. 'Thanks for coming, John,' she said gently, 'I hope you have fun here. And if it gets to be too much, just come back to the hotel and swim in the pool.'

'Don't worry about me. I'm looking forward to it, Fiona.'

'Good. I'll see you downstairs.' She hung up quickly, and predictably it was seven-thirty when he saw her hurrying through the lobby. There were a million people milling around, or so it seemed, the usual summer tourists who stayed at the Ritz and came from everywhere and those who had come for the haute couture. There were models, photographers, editors, reporters, clients of haute couture wearing their prizes from the last shows in January, European, American, Arab, and Asian women, with their husbands in tow, and a crowd of gawkers staring at them all. And outside the hotel there were groupies and paparazzi waiting to snap photographs of anyone well known. According to the whispers in the crowd, Madonna had just cruised through moments before. Like most of the other stars staying in the hotel, they were going to the Dior show. Moments later Fiona and John slipped into the chauffeured car she'd hired for her stay, and they sped off toward the station. Adrian and both their assistants were following in a separate car. Their photographers

73

were already at the train station, and had been set up there for hours. The shots they got were all important. The haute couture shows in Paris were the World Series of Fashion.

As Fiona glanced over at him, she smiled in amusement. 'I can't believe you're doing this with me. You're a hell of a good sport, John.'

'Just ignorant, I guess. I have no idea what I'm getting into.' But it already seemed like fun to him. He loved the atmosphere and the underlying sense of tension and anticipation. 'How are they going to do this in a train station?' They were headed toward the Gare d'Austerlitz.

'God knows. We'll see. If I lose you after the show, find the car outside, or meet me back at the hotel.' She was anticipating barely controlled chaos, which was an appropriate assumption at almost any of the shows.

'Do you want to pin my address to my shirt? My mother did that once when we went to Disneyland. She had absolutely no confidence in my ability to remember my own name. She was right of course. I got lost as soon as we got there.'

'Just don't forget mine,' she said with a rueful grin as they got out of the car, and fought their way through the crowd. Their VIP tickets were large silver cardboard invitations that were easy to spot, but in spite of that, it took them nearly twenty minutes to fight their way through. It was after eight by the time they got in, and were taken to leopard-printed directors' chairs set up on the platform. The chairs seemed to stretch as far as the eye could see. And the theme was, as Fiona already knew, African jungle.

It was eight-thirty when they finally started the show. The entire train station where they sat went dark, and an antique train came slowly toward them, as what seemed like a thousand drums began beating in the pulsating rhythms of the jungle, and a hundred men dressed as Masai warriors appeared from nowhere and stood glaring at them. When the lights came back on, it was awesome, and John was watching it in fascination. He had already spotted Catherine Deneuve, Madonna and her entourage, and the queen of Jordan sitting nearby. They were in impressive company, and John alternated between watching what was happening and keeping an eye on Fiona. She sat quiet and still, concentrating on what was coming, and within instants, it began to happen, as the music got louder, and three men with two tigers and a snow leopard walked slowly through the crowd. And as she saw them, Fiona smiled.

'This,' she said with a look at John, 'is pure Dior.' The only thing missing was an elephant, and within moments, one arrived with two handlers and a huge rhinestone-covered saddle. John couldn't help wondering if the animals were likely to panic in the crowd, but no one seemed to care, they were waiting with bated breath for the clothes, which came next.

Each model was preceded and followed by a Masai warrior, in authentic dress, with spears, and scars, and heavily painted. And each model was exquisite, as one by one they stepped off the train. The clothes were beaded, colorful, exotic, with long sweeping painted taffeta skirts, or lace leggings covered with beads, extraordinary intricately beaded bustiers, or some stepped off the train with their breasts bare, as John tried not to stare. In fact, one of them walked straight up to John, enveloped in a huge embroidered coat, and slowly opened it, unveiling her flawless body, wearing only a G-string, as Fiona watched with amusement. The models loved playing with the crowd. John fought valiantly to appear calm and not squirm in his chair as the model walked away. It had been an unforgettable moment. And all the while, Fiona sat watching the girls file past with an unreadable expression, which was part of her mystique. She had a well-trained poker face that allowed no one to guess if she approved of the clothes or not. She would let the world know what she thought when she was ready to and not before. And John didn't ask her. He loved watching her, and the proceedings.

The evening gowns that came toward the end of the show were equally fabulous and unique. He couldn't imagine any of the women he knew wearing these creations to the opening of the Met, or any of the events he went to, but he loved watching them, and seeing all the drama and spectacle that surrounded the models. And when the bride came out, she was wearing a huge exaggerated version of a Masai headdress, a white painted taffeta skirt so enormous she could hardly get it off the train, and a gold breastplate entirely encrusted with diamonds. And at the instant the model stepped off the train, John Galliano appeared on a white elephant, wearing a loincloth, and an identical breastplate himself. And half a dozen of the painted warriors lifted the bride up to him, and sat her behind him on the elephant, as they both waved and were led away. The tigers and snow leopard had been removed by then, which seemed fortunate to John, as the crowd around them went absolutely berserk, screaming and shouting and cheering and applauding, as the rest of the models filed past, and the drum music got deafeningly louder. And moments later the warriors and models got on the train, and were carried out of the station. It was pandemonium on the platform, as Fiona finally turned to look at John.

'Well?' She looked amused, and could see that he was stunned. He had been mesmerized by the performance. It was heady stuff for a novice, or even an aficionado of the couture shows. But in this realm at least, John was decidedly a virgin. This was a hell of a way to go.

'Just another day at the office for you, I guess.' He smiled at her. He had loved it. 'But it blew my socks off. Absolutely amazing. All of it. The clothes, the women, the warriors, the music, the animals. I didn't know where to look first.' In a far, far more glamorous way, it had reminded him of his first time at a three-ring circus. This wasn't even Disneyland. It was nirvana. 'Is it always like this?'

'At Dior it is. They seem to outdo themselves every time. The old houses never did anything like this. The shows used to be elegant and sedate. But Dior has been this way ever since Galliano. It's more about theater than fashion. It's more of a publicity campaign than a serious intent to dress women. But it works for them, and the press loves it.'

'Does anyone wear the clothes?' He couldn't imagine it, although a wedding with Galliano's bride in the gold and diamond breastplate would have been interesting certainly.

'Not many. And they make a lot of changes and adjustments. There are only thirty or forty women in the world who wear couture anyway, so many of the houses are closing. The workmanship is so intense, the cost of the materials and labor so high, they all lose money on it. Which is why in some cases they make it about publicity now and not making money. But in some ways, it has an impact on ready-to-wear, and it's worth covering from that standpoint. Because sooner or later, we'll see some mutation of this on real women who buy their clothes at Barney's.'

'I can hardly wait for that,' John said, and she laughed. 'I'd love to see that at my office.'

'You might at some point, in a very watered-down version. Sooner or later it gets there, in a forum and rendition tolerable to the masses. This is where it starts, in its purest form.' It was one way to look at it, and he knew she was intensely knowledgeable about her business. He had even more respect for her, and was even more fascinated by her, after seeing her in Paris. And she was obviously enjoying being with him.

As the crowd began to thin, they made their way toward the exits. They were going back to the hotel for a drink, and eventually they were going to a public swimming pool for the party hosted by Dior. But Fiona said there was no point going before midnight. It was already ten o'clock as they left the station. And ten-thirty when they got back to the hotel, and they settled in at a corner table in the bar for cocktails and hors d'oeuvres. He was starving by then, but she said she wasn't hungry. Adrian stopped in to see them for a few minutes, said he thought the show was fabulous, and every five minutes, someone else stopped to say hello to Fiona. It was more than obvious that in this realm she was queen.

'Do you ever get a break from all this?' he asked with interest.

'Not here,' she said, sipping a glass of white wine. He had ordered a martini, and he didn't complain to her that it was mostly vermouth. He didn't really care. He was having too much fun with her to care what he drank. And it was easy to see how much she loved it, not just the attention,

79

but the ambiance. She was totally in her element, surrounded by her subjects and slaves. Everyone wanted to know what she thought of the clothes, and she was ready to admit finally that she loved them for the most part.

'What did you love about them?' he asked, intrigued.

'The workmanship, the detail, the imagination, the color, the mood. The painted skirts were fabulous, they were works of art. He really is a genius. You know, in haute couture, every single stitch in any garment must be sewn by hand. There isn't a single machine stitch in the entire collection,' she explained. It was all a mystery to John. It was about as far as you could get from the world of the little black cocktail dress that he understood. It was Fiona's world, not his. And he admired her for it. 'Do you like clothes?' she asked as they munched nuts, and little hors d'oeuvres, while exotic-looking people continued to interrupt them. They were all paying homage to Fiona, and some seemed curious about John when she introduced him. But most ignored him. It was Fiona they wanted to talk to, and approached in droves.

'I like well-dressed women. This is a little beyond me, but it certainly is fun to watch. And very different.' She nodded, as yet another hanger-on stopped at their table. 'You don't get much peace here.' In fact she got none at all. But she hadn't come to Paris for peace.

'I don't expect to,' she said calmly. The truth was she didn't get much peace anywhere, and didn't mind it. This was what she had filled her life with instead of a husband and children. The only constants in her life were her work, Adrian, and Sir Winston. The rest was stage sets and actors who came and went onstage. She loved the visuals and the drama. 'I think too much peace makes me nervous. I miss the noise.'

'How are you on vacation?' he asked with interest. It was hard to imagine her doing nothing, or alone. She seemed so much a part of the chaos she lived in, he could no longer imagine her without it, nor could she. He suspected that long term, or full time, it would drive him crazy, but it totally fascinated him for now.

'I get anxious for the first week,' she said honestly in answer to his question. 'And bored the second.' They both laughed at what she'd said.

'And the third?'

'I go back to work.'

'That's what I thought. So no taking a month off on a desert island. That's too bad.'

'I spent a month in Tahiti once after I'd been sick, and my doctor insisted I go to a warm climate and rest. I nearly went out of my mind. I take my vacations in Paris, London, and New York.'

'And St. Tropez,' he added, and she smiled.

'That's more of this, with water and bikinis. It's not really peace. But it's a lot of fun.' He conceded that it would be, especially with her. She was a rare, exotic bird, with plumage as bright and colorful as what he had just seen at Dior – there was nothing small and brown and tame about her. Nothing at all. But he liked her this way. Immensely so. 'Are you ready for another round of Dior?' she inquired with a look of mischief.

'More tigers and elephants and warriors?' They were intriguing, but he had had enough of them for one day.

'No, it's a water theme,' Fiona told him, but once again, when they arrived, he was completely bowled over by what they had done to an ordinary swimming pool. There was a Lucite dance floor placed over the pool, with huge exotic fish swimming under it, and girls painted to look like fish in brilliant hues with stripes of gold wearing only body paint and nothing else as they wandered through the crowd. And men in tiny gold bikinis with incredible bodies served food and drinks. The techno music was deafening as people danced and writhed on the Lucite floor. The entire party was decorated to look as though it were underwater. They served sushi and exotic seafood, and every supermodel in Paris was there, along with movie stars, photographers, socialites, aristocracy and royalty, exquisite people, and the elite of the fashion world. And again everyone knew Fiona and greeted her. It was an incredible evening, but John was grateful when they left in less than an hour. Fiona had done her duty and was satisfied to leave, as they both leaned back against the seat in the limousine, relieved to have escaped the noise.

'My God, that was quite a scene,' he said, unable to find words to comment on it. He was beginning to feel like Alice in Wonderland, or as though he had overdosed on LSD at lunch. He couldn't imagine spending a week doing this twice a year, but she seemed to thrive on it, and be unperturbed by the frenzy and turmoil. She smiled peacefully at him as they drove back to the Ritz under an incredibly beautiful Paris night sky.

'The other parties this week won't be as exotic as this. Dior goes all out.' She knew they had spent three million dollars on the party they'd just left and much more on the show they'd seen that afternoon. The other houses were more circumspect, both in their budgets and their themes. This was quite an introduction for him, and as they approached the Place Vendôme, Fiona asked the driver to stop and turned to John. 'Do you want to walk for a few minutes, or are you too tired?' She liked walking in Paris before she went home to bed, but it had been a long day for both of them, and jet lag was finally catching up with her.

'I'd like that,' he said quietly, as she dismissed the car for the night, and they strolled slowly down the rue Castiglione to the Place Vendôme. Suddenly they felt like real people in a real world in the most beautiful city on the planet, and he was grateful for the exercise and the air. It seemed to restore some normalcy to the night after all the exotic things they'd experienced and seen. 'I was beginning to feel like I was on drugs,' he admitted, as they walked into the square, and stopped to look in shop windows. He felt almost normal again, just tired.

'Have you had enough of it?' Fiona asked, curious about the extent of his tolerance for her milieu.

'Not yet. I'm fascinated, although today will be hard to top. I'm going to be disappointed, I think, if the other shows are anything less.'

'Not less, just more restrained. You might enjoy them more. They're not as much sensory overload as Dior. That's their stock-in-trade.'

'And yours?' he asked, as he tucked her hand in his arm and they walked on.

'Maybe. I like the beautiful and the exotic, interesting people with talent and creative spirits. I think I've gotten spoiled. Sometimes I'm not sure what normal is anymore. This is all normal to me. I forget sometimes that other people lead simpler lives.'

'You're going to be very bored if you leave all this one day, Fiona. Or maybe it will give you something exciting to write about.' But even after knowing her for such a short time, he could not imagine her doing anything other than what she was, with a flock of adoring minions revolving around her. It was heady air she breathed, and in the midst of it all, she was the queen bee, as powerful as any queen. He imagined it made it hard for her to ally with any man – and he was sure she was well aware of it. Few men would be willing to exist on the fringes of her world. And fewer still would be able or willing to participate in it. To most men, her life was like traveling on a rocket through outer space. And John felt that way too. But he enjoyed being with her, it was a rare opportunity. But not one he could have tolerated easily day to day. His own life seemed half-dead and incredibly mundane compared with hers, although he ran one of the largest ad agencies in the world. But even his world seemed tame compared to hers. He couldn't even begin to imagine what it would be like being married to her. And he wondered now if this was why she had never married, and he couldn't resist asking her as they approached the Ritz. He wondered if her single life was too much fun to give up and married life far too boring. He couldn't imagine anyone with a husband or wife staying in that world for long.

'Not really,' she said thoughtfully. 'I've just never felt a need to be married, nor wanted to be. It seems so painful when it doesn't work out. I've never wanted to take that risk. Rather like jumping out of a burning building. If you're lucky, you might land in the net they hold out to you, but from what I can see, you're a lot more likely to hit the cement.' She looked at him with wide honest eyes, and he laughed, as they walked slowly into the Ritz. There were guards with dogs outside.

And the paparazzi were still standing watch, waiting for celebrities to come home.

'That's one way to look at it, I guess. It's wonderful when it does work out. I loved being married. But you have to choose the right person, and maybe have a lot of luck.' They both thought of his late wife as he said it, although Fiona didn't want to go there.

'I've never liked gambling,' Fiona said honestly. 'I'd rather spend my money on things I like, than risk losing it all. And I've never met anyone who I thought would really be able to tolerate being part of my life forever. I travel a lot, I'm too busy, I have a lot of crazy people around. My dog snores. And I like it all just the way it is.' Somehow, John found that hard to believe. In his mind, sooner or later, everyone realizes that they don't want to be alone. And yet, he had to admit that she seemed immensely content with her life just as it was.

'And what happens when you get old?'

'I'll deal with it. I've always thought that was a particularly stupid reason to get married. Why spend thirty years with someone who makes you uncomfortable, in order not to be alone when you get old? What if I got Alzheimer's and didn't even remember him? Think of all the time I'd have wasted being miserable, in order not to be unhappy when I'm old. That's like an insurance policy, not a union of minds and souls. Besides, I could go down in a plane next week, and then I'd make someone terribly unhappy if something like that happened. This way the only one who'd be upset is my dog.' John found it an odd way to look at things, but she seemed comfortable with it.

It was the antithesis of the way he'd lived, with a long marriage, a wife he had loved, and two kids. And even though he'd been devastated when Ann died, he thought the years they'd shared before were well worth it. When he went, he wanted to be mourned by more than a dog. But Fiona didn't. She was very clear about it. She had seen her mother's pain each time a man left her life, and felt her own when her two long-term relationships had ended. She could only imagine that marriage, and losing a spouse, would be far worse, perhaps even unbearable. It was easier, in her mind at least, not to have one in the first place. So she filled her life with other things, pastimes, pursuits, projects, and people.

'Besides,' she continued thoughtfully, 'I don't like being encumbered. Maybe I just like my freedom.' She grinned impishly at him as she shrugged her shoulders, but she did so without apology. 'My life suits me as it is.' And in spite of his own very different ideas, he agreed with her. She seemed perfectly content with her existence, and made no bones about it.

Once back in the Ritz, they walked past the vitrines full of expensive items of jewelry and clothing, as he took her to the elevator on the Cambon side. Their rooms were on the third floor, and his was just down the hall from hers. He stood outside her door, as she reached into her bag to find the large blue plastic key. They put it on a heavy brass ring, and she always took the key off and left the brass part on the desk in her room. It was too heavy to drag around in her bag. John waited politely until she found it, inserted it in the electronic lock, and the door opened as she turned to thank him for coming to Paris with her. It had been fun sharing the Dior evening with him, from beginning to end. Or rather, from train station to pool.

'Do you have time for breakfast tomorrow morning, or will you be too busy?' he asked, as she noticed that he looked as impeccably groomed as he had at the beginning of the evening. And it was already two o'clock in the morning. It had been a long night, but a good one. And he wore well. He was flexible and easygoing and fun to be with, and he had a nice manly look to him that she was not unaware of. She just wasn't ready to respond to it. Or at least she was being careful not to for the time being.

'I have to make some calls when I get up, and at some point, I have to meet with our photographer to go over the proof sheets from the Dior show. But he won't have them until late afternoon. And we have to be at the Lacroix show at eleven. We should leave here at ten-thirty . . . I want to dress by nine . . . I could do breakfast with you at eight-thirty.' She made it sound like a business meeting she was fitting in, and he smiled at her.

'I think I can manage that.' He had to make some business calls himself, but he was planning to do them in the afternoon, because of the time difference with New York. 'What do you like for breakfast? I'll order for both of us, if that's all right with you.' She was so independent that he didn't want to step on her toes, or make her feel out of control. He had a feeling that wouldn't be a good move.

'Grapefruit and coffee,' she said unceremoniously, with a small yawn. She was getting sleepy, and he liked the way she looked when she did. She seemed somehow softer and smaller, and not quite as efficient or as daunting, or as much in control.

'Can't you do better than that? You can't run around till lunchtime on half a grapefruit and a cup of coffee. You'll fall over, Fiona. What about an omelette?' She looked hesitant for a minute, and then nodded. 'Do you like anything in it?'

'Chanterelles,' she said, smiling up at him, and he looked pleased.

'That sounds good to me too. I'll order it for eight-thirty. My room or yours?' But he had already guessed before she said it. He was starting to know her.

'Mine probably. Someone may need to call me. I'm working.'

'No problem. See you in the morning, Fiona. I had a wonderful time tonight. Thank you for including me. This is definitely a night I won't forget, though I don't think anyone would believe me if I described it to them. I think I liked all those Masai warriors best of all.'

'Naturally.' She smiled at him. 'That's boy stuff.'

'What did you like best?' he asked with interest.

She had a sudden overwhelming urge to say 'being with you' but didn't, and was shocked at herself that it had even come to mind. 'The wedding dress maybe, or the painted skirts.' She was going to write about them for the magazine, and hoped that the photographs of them were good.

'I thought the tigers and leopard were great too,' he said, sounding boyish. He could hardly wait to tell his daughters what he'd seen. They knew he had gone to Paris, but they didn't know why or with whom. He always let his daughters know where he was, particularly now that Ann was gone.

'I should have taken you to the natural history museum or the zoo instead of Dior,' Fiona teased him, and they both laughed, as she scolded him for the irreverence, and lack of fascination with fashion, but she knew he'd had a good time, which was all that mattered. They lingered for a moment, sensing each other more than saying anything, and then he gently kissed her on the forehead and walked to his own room with a wave. Fiona felt haunted by him as she walked into her own room. He was damnably attractive, responsible and normal, sensible and so undeniably all-male. For a mad moment, she wanted to run down the hall after him, but she had no idea what she would do after that, if she did. She was trying to keep her head clear despite his proximity, but suddenly it seemed harder to do. She felt overwhelmingly attracted to him. But fortunately, he had closed the door to his room by then, and Fiona congratulated herself silently for her self-control. It would serve no purpose getting involved with him, she told herself. She had made that decision in the course of the evening. He was handsome as hell, and she was physically attracted to him, but she was wise enough to know that they were just too different. She wasn't a kid anymore, after all, and some gifts, no matter how alluring they were, were better left wrapped and unopened. All she had to do now was get through the next few days of the shows without losing control. She was determined to do just that and not succumb to John's charm, no matter how hard to do. And when it came to self-control, Fiona was a pro.

5

John Anderson knocked on Fiona's door the next morning, with the room service waiter standing right behind him. As Fiona opened the door, she looked wide awake and was wearing a pink terry-cloth Ritz robe and matching slippers. Her teeth were brushed, her hair was combed, and she told John she had been on the phone since seven o'clock that morning. She and Adrian had discussed the Dior show from the day before, and were in complete agreement as to which were the most important pieces. They were both going to Lacroix that morning. Adrian had been to the *ateliers* the day before and was extremely enthusiastic about what they'd shown him. By the time John arrived for breakfast, her head was already full of business and fashion.

'Did you sleep well?' he asked solicitously. He was wearing gray slacks and a blue shirt with the collar open. And he was wearing impeccably shined black Gucci loafers. As she looked at him, she was aware once again of how attractive and sexy she found him.

'Yes, thank you.' She smiled at him as the waiter set out their breakfast on the rolling table and pulled up two comfortable chairs for them. There was a folded newspaper at each place, and a small vase of red roses on the table. It was the perfect breakfast. 'I always sleep well. Although I have to admit, after I've been here awhile, I miss the sound of Sir Winston snoring. It's kind of like the ocean,' she said as they both sat down, and glanced at the papers. They had two copies of the *Herald Tribune*. And for a moment, they sat in silence, eating, lost in their own thoughts, as they contemplated the morning.

'So what am I going to see today? More leopards and tigers, or something tamer?'

'Today you see living art.' She smiled at him. 'Poetry in motion. Living sculpture. Lacroix's clothes are like paintings worn by women, with different elements integrated, unrelated fabrics, and vibrant colors. I think you'll love it.'

'Anything like yesterday?' he asked with interest, sitting back in his chair, eyeing her. He liked the way she looked in the morning with her hair cascading past her shoulders. It made her look younger. She thought he had the clean, fresh-shaven look of a man of distinction and good grooming, and even from across the table, she noticed that he smelled delicious.

'Completely different,' she said, in answer to his question. 'This is quiet, distinguished, striking, but very elegant. Galliano is a showman and creates theater, Lacroix is a genius and creates art.'

'I like your description,' John said, turning to the financial page of the paper, and glancing down the list of stocks. Once satisfied that all was well, he turned his attention back to her. 'You're teaching me a lot.' He wasn't sure what he'd do with it, but he liked sharing the experience with her. It was fun seeing her in her world, and getting to know her better.

She ate the whole omelette he had ordered for her, the half grapefruit she had wanted anyway, and then as an afterthought, she ate a *pain au chocolat* and drank two cups of coffee. 'I can't see you anymore, John,' she said as she set her cup down, and he looked across the table at her, startled.

'That was sudden.' He suddenly wondered if there was someone else in her life. It would explain the distance he felt from her occasionally. He had thought it was self-protection, and now he wondered if it was actually due to another romance. He hated to admit it, but he was disappointed. 'What brought that on?'

'Breakfast. If I hang around you any longer, I'll be the size of this table. You're too fattening. I eat too much when I'm with you.' He looked at her in amazement and relief and grinned broadly. And then sounded sheepish when he answered.

'I thought you meant it. For a minute you had me worried.' He felt vulnerable as he said it.

'I did mean it. I can't afford to get fat in my business. I'd look foolish. I mean, how chic is a two-hundred-pound editor of the world's most important fashion magazine? They'd drum me right out of the business, and it would be all your fault.'

'Okay, in that case, stop eating. I'm not going to feed you ever again, and if I see you touch lunch today, we'll call the doctor and ask him to have your stomach stapled. Personally, I think you could use a little weight, but who am I to ask you to risk your job for an omelette?'

'It's not the omelette, it's the *pain au chocolat* that went with it. I'm addicted to them.' She was smiling at him as she said it, and just looking at her, he could feel a tug at his heart.

'We'll put you in a twelve-step program when you get home. But I still think you need to eat breakfast.' And the truth was that she was enjoying every moment of eating it with him. He was good company, even in the morning, and usually she didn't like talking to anyone before she got to the office, even Sir Winston. But this was different. This was Paris, and there was an aura of ease and happiness and romance everywhere around them. Particularly at the Ritz. It was one of her favorite hotels in the world. Ordinarily, when he came to town, he stayed at the Crillon. But this time he was happy to be at the Ritz, with her.

'I have to get dressed,' she said unceremoniously and stood up, in bare feet and the pink bathrobe.

And for a moment, he felt nearly married, whatever her views on the subject. They were in the
living room of her suite.

'You look very pretty.'

'Like this?' She looked at him as though he had
said something utterly ridiculous, as she ran a
hand through her hair and tightened the bathrobe.
She was wearing nothing underneath it, but he
couldn't see anything, and the pale pink color
looked soft and flattering near her face. 'Don't be
silly,' she said, dismissing the compliment, walked
into her bedroom, and closed the door. He said he
was going to read the paper while he waited, but
instead when she returned, she found him staring
out the window. He was lost in thought, and gave
a start when she touched his shoulder. He had
been a million miles away, and thinking of her.

'Don't you look elegant,' he said admiringly. She
was wearing a black-and-white summer linen
pantsuit that had been given to her the year before
as a gift from Balmain, and it suited her well. She
was wearing high-heeled black lizard Blahnik
sandals, and a soft black leather Hermès bag
known as the 'Kelly mou.' Her hair was tied back
in a neat knot, and she was wearing big black shell
earrings by Seaman Schepps. She looked elegant
and demure, and the only spot of color was her
enormous turquoise bracelet on her wrist. She
looked every bit the editor-in-chief of *Chic*.
'Ready?' he asked as they prepared to leave the
room. It was all very proper, but somehow felt

surprisingly domestic, and as they walked out of the living room of her suite, they ran right into Adrian, hurrying out of his room. He raised an eyebrow at both of them and grinned.

'My, my, isn't this good news. I was hoping something like that would happen. A honeymoon at the Ritz.' It was a rather bold assumption on his part.

'Oh, shut up, Adrian,' Fiona said, looking embarrassed, as John smiled at them both. He had put on a blazer by then, and a good-looking yellow Hermès tie. 'We just had breakfast together. Relax. I'm still a virgin.'

'That's disappointing to hear,' he said as they got in the elevator together. John seemed to be a good sport about Adrian's teasing. The two men chatted on the way down, and Fiona strode out of the elevator ahead of them. As it turned out, Adrian's driver was late, so all three of them rode to the Académie des Beaux Arts on the Left Bank together in Fiona's car.

And just as Fiona had predicted, the show was dignified, yet elegant and impressive, an entirely different scene than the show she'd taken John to the day before. He was vastly impressed and said he loved it. After the show, Adrian went back to the hotel to talk to the photographer. John and Fiona went to lunch at Le Voltaire. She was beginning to feel as though she were being lazy. She was more interested in spending time with John than in doing her work.

They shared a relaxing, comfortable three hours eating lunch at Le Voltaire, and by the time it was full, Fiona knew more than half the people there. Hubert de Givenchy had come for lunch, as did the Baronne de Ludinghausen, formerly from Saint Laurent. There were designers and socialites and bankers, and as they ordered coffee, Fiona chatted amiably with a Russian prince at the next table. She knew everyone, and more important, they all knew her.

They both went back to the hotel to make phone calls to New York after lunch, and met up again at four-thirty. They had agreed to take a walk down the Faubourg St. Honoré, and he followed her willingly into Hermès. By the time they got back to the hotel at six o'clock, they had spent the entire day together, and Fiona was surprised at how totally at ease she felt with him. It was so comfortable being together. She went to change, while he sent some e-mails on his computer, and when they met again an hour later, she was wearing an ice-blue silk suit. They were on their way to see Givenchy, which turned out to be slightly outrageous, and although she said she liked some of the pieces, she was disappointed in it from a professional point of view.

After that they came back to the Ritz for the *Chic* magazine cocktail party, which Adrian had in total control. Everyone who was anyone was there. Fiona made the rounds greeting people and shaking hands. It was hours later when she and John left for the last of the Givenchy party, which was a spectacular event in a tent in the Luxembourg Garden. And at midnight they went to the Buddha Bar for a few minutes, because she'd promised to meet some people there. Then they stopped at the Hemingway Bar at the hotel for a last drink. John had brandy and she had mineral water, and she realized in amazement that it was two-thirty in the morning by the time they left the bar and went upstairs. Things always started late in Paris, and as a result, the nights got late.

'Is it always like this when you come to the couture shows?' he asked as they rode up in the elevator together. He hated to admit it, but he was exhausted. She led life at a pace that would have killed him in a week. It was a lot easier, he realized, going to an office and having sedate dinners out a couple of times a week. He couldn't even begin to think of all the things they had done and seen in two days. And she didn't even look tired as she fumbled in her bag for her key.

'Yes, it's always pretty hectic.' She smiled at him. 'Do you want a day off tomorrow? I'm going to Chanel in the morning, and Gaultier in the afternoon.' As though that meant something to him. She might as well have been speaking Chinese. But he liked the sound of it on her lips.

'I wouldn't miss it for anything. I'm getting an education, or something like that.' And then suddenly he wondered if it was awkward for her

99

to be seen constantly with him. That possibility hadn't even occurred to him. This wasn't a pleasure cruise for her after all, it was a business trip. 'Would you rather go alone, Fiona?' He looked worried, and she smiled at him, leaning against the doorway of her suite. They felt like old friends now, and she was astonishingly at ease with him.

'I'd rather go with you,' she said honestly. 'You make it more fun for me. It's almost like doing something new.' It was a nice thing to say to him, and without saying a word, he gently touched her cheek.

'I like being with you too.' Even more than he had dreamed. It had been a memorable two days with her, and without thinking, he leaned slowly toward her, and the next thing he knew, he was holding her and kissing her in the doorway of her suite. They stood there for a long time, and the thought crossed John's mind that Adrian might happen by on the way to his room. But he didn't want to force his way into Fiona's room. So they stood there kissing, and holding each other, until she spoke in a soft, smoky voice, and whispered in his ear.

'Would you like to come in?'

'I thought you'd never ask,' he whispered back, and she giggled, as they walked into the living room and closed the door softly behind them. And for a moment they both felt like two naughty kids who had given their parents the slip.

'Would you like a drink?' she asked, as she stepped out of her shoes, and stood in front of him in bare feet. She had taken off her suit jacket at the bar, and was wearing a peach satin camisole that was slipping enticingly off one shoulder. All he could think of was Fiona, the last thing he wanted was a drink. 'No, my love, I don't want a drink,' he said as he took her in his arms again, and a moment later the satin camisole had slid obligingly to her waist, and all he could feel was the delicious silk of her skin.

She took his hand then, and he followed her into her bedroom. The bed was turned down impeccably, as though it were waiting for a royal couple, and as he kissed her again, he flicked off the light, and followed her to her bed. And in the darkness, his clothes disappeared as quickly as hers did, and a moment later they were in bed, lying in each other's arms for a long time, and savoring the moment, and then, as though a tidal wave had hit them, passion overwhelmed them both. It was a long, delicious night that neither of them had hoped for, or dreamed of, but if either of them had ever had a dream, the night they spent together would have been it.

6

Fiona attempted to look respectable and solemn as they left for Chanel the next morning. John was wearing a gray suit, a white shirt, and a midnight blue tie and looked as though he were going to a business meeting. And as if to compensate for her follies of the night before, Fiona wore a serious black Chanel suit, with a short skirt. But all she managed to achieve was to look sexier than ever. At least he thought so, as he wrapped his arms around her, and held her tightly against him as the elevator at the Ritz made its way to the Cambon lobby, and Fiona giggled.

'You're in good spirits this morning,' he teased her. They both were. With good reason. It had been a remarkable night for both of them.

'I was just thinking of the cameras in the elevator. We could really give them something to look at,' she said with another giggle, but by then the doors had opened, and there was a Japanese family waiting to get in. John followed Fiona out and straightened his tie. They both felt as though the entire world could see what had happened the night before. It seemed so obvious to them. 'Is my skirt too short?' she asked, looking worried, as one of the security men let them out through the ordinarily locked Cambon door. They opened it only for her, because then it was just a short walk across the street to Chanel. Otherwise they would have had to go all the way around the Place Vendôme, which made no sense.

'I think your skirt should be shorter,' John said in an undertone as they reached Chanel. There were crowds of people outside, waiting to get in, and the usual group of paparazzi and legitimate photographers. The House of Chanel was small, and the group that attended the couture show was select and elite. The moment they saw Fiona, they made a path for her in the crowd and let her in. She took John by the arm, and he walked in beside her, as photographers snapped pictures of both of them. 'Is that all right?' he asked softly, he didn't want to create a problem for her. She was well-known after all, and he didn't know if she minded being photographed with a man. But she smiled at the camera, and then up at him.

'It's fine. You look terrific,' she said, and then walked sedately up the stairs, and a moment later they took their seats.

Unlike the other shows, Chanel started punctually, and the clothes were respectable and terrific. They played Mozart as the models made their way sedately down the designated path through the seats. Every aspect of the show was about elegance and tradition. It was like visiting a grande dame for tea. Karl Lagerfeld had designed a collection that knocked everyone off their feet. The wedding gown at the end was every bit as spectacular as Adrian had told her it would be. The velvet gown with the ermine cape caused everyone to catch their breath, and Lagerfeld himself got a standing ovation when he appeared. Fiona knew the press would go wild with the photographs, and she could hardly wait to print them in *Chic*. The wedding dress was absolutely exquisite, as the whole collection had been.

'It's a shame it has to be a wedding dress,' John said, as they wended their way through the crowd on the way out. Fiona had stopped for a moment to say hello to Karl, and she had introduced John to him. 'It would look incredible on you.' Fiona couldn't help laughing as she smiled at him.

'Thank you for the compliment, and I haven't seen the prices yet, but roughly speaking, that dress probably costs about as much as a small summer cottage. And they don't give dresses like that to editors for free.'

'Too bad, it would be great on you,' he said sincerely.

They were still laughing and chatting when they were let back into the hotel by the security, and had lunch in the garden. After that they hurried to Gaultier with Adrian. Gaultier was his favorite show, and exactly his cup of tea. The entire collection was red this year, including the fur coats, and the theme of the whole collection was Chinese. It was extremely dramatic, but Fiona was less enthused.

The last collection they went to late that afternoon was Valentino's, and it was as elegant as Chanel had been. And as always, Valentino had done a lot with red too. For once even Fiona was tired when they got back to the hotel. She had a million notes and photographs to go through, but she was going to do that in the morning, after John left. For their last night, they had agreed to have dinner at a simple restaurant on a Bateau Mouche and wanted to walk around the Left Bank afterward. And the day after John left, she was going to St. Tropez. Adrian was planning to head back to New York when she did. He had a lot to do. The aftermath of the Paris couture shows always kept them busy for weeks. It was rare for her, but Fiona had decided to go on vacation for two full weeks. She hadn't taken that much time off in years, but felt she needed it.

'You look tired, do you want a cup of tea?' John asked solicitously. She nodded gratefully, happy to collapse on the couch for a while as she went through her messages. The night before had been short, and they hadn't gotten much sleep. He ordered tea for himself too, and they sat relaxing on the couch, talking about the three shows they'd seen that day, and she congratulated him for seeing every important show in couture week.

105

'Thanks to you. I wouldn't even know how to describe it to anyone. It was incredible, Fiona.' And then he leaned over and kissed her. 'And so are you.' He hadn't been this happy in years, and had never known anyone like her. She was magical and exciting and fascinating and mysterious all at once. She was like a beautiful animal in the wild, running free, but so unforgettably beautiful and enticing when she stopped to look at you. He was head over heels in love with her and had only known her for a matter of weeks. Fiona was astounded by it, and it amazed him too. She was just as crazy about him. But she was afraid it was just a phenomenon of Paris, and the excitement of the trip. She was afraid that once they got home, it would break the spell, and she said as much to him as they drank their tea.

'Don't be so cynical, Fiona,' he chided her. 'Don't you think you can fall in love at our age? People do it all the time. People a lot older than we are. Why shouldn't this be real?'

'What if it isn't?' she said, looking worried. She wanted it to be. More than she had wanted anything in years. She had never known anyone like him either. Strong, solid, sensible, warm, affectionate, intelligent, kind, reasonable, and he seemed perfectly able to tolerate the occasional insanity of her career, even during couture week. He liked Adrian, who was a mainstay in her life. She was not entirely certain of the future of the relationship between him and Sir Winston, but that could be worked on. The rest seemed perfect, although she knew nothing was, and this couldn't be. But it sure looked it. He seemed to be everything she had ever wanted all rolled into one human being. Her dream prince, and he was not only handsome but distinguished and sexy, and very intelligent too. They had chemistry galore.

'Don't be such a scaredy-cat,' he said confidently. He also wanted her to meet his children. He was sure his girls were going to love her, if only because he did.

'I'm going to miss you when I go to St. Tropez,' she said, nibbling a cookie. Now she was sorry that she was going. It was going to be boring and lonely without him. And she had gotten a message the day before that the friends who were meeting her with their boat were stuck in Sardinia, due to bad weather and rough seas, and they had decided to stay there. So she was going to be on her own at the Hotel Byblos in St. Tropez.

'We could do something about that, if you want to. But I don't want to intrude on your vacation, Fiona. You need it. And you'll only be gone for two weeks.' It seemed like an eternity to him too.

'What did you have in mind?' she asked with interest.

'It sounds a little crazy, but if you'd like, I can reshuffle some meetings. At this time of year, almost everyone is on vacation. And my girls are busy. If you want, I could come with you. But if you'd rather not, I understand perfectly. I can keep busy for the next two weeks.' But she was already beaming at him.

'Would you do that? Could you?' It was a crazy thing to do, she knew, but she didn't care. She was loving being with him, and she wanted to go to St. Tropez with him, if he could arrange it.

'I could, would, and would love to. Does it sound good to you too?'

'It sounds terrific,' she assured him.

He called his secretary half an hour later, while Fiona showered and dressed for the evening. She emerged wearing beige silk slacks and a little beige silk sweater that you could almost see through, but not quite. She always managed to look elegant and sexy, and she was wearing little red silk mules for their informal evening on the Bateau Mouche.

'Could she do it?' Fiona asked, like a kid waiting for Christmas, referring to his change of plans, and he laughed at the question.

'I didn't give her a choice, I told her she had to. It's a little crazy, but what the hell, Fiona, you only live once. Who knows when we'll get the chance to do this again, we're both so damn busy. You've already got the time off, the least I can do is arrange my schedule to suit you.' He was smiling at her, sitting on the bed in the bedroom of her suite, and she put her arms around him, grateful to have found him, and to be with him.

'You are truly amazing.' But it was he who thought she was.

An hour later they were on the Bateau Mouche

eating steak and *pommes frites* for dinner, and drifting along the Seine, looking at the lights and monuments of Paris. It was a corny, touristy thing to do, but the idea had appealed to both of them, and they were delighted they'd done it. They were talking about their plans for St. Tropez, and John wanted to call a boat broker he knew to see if he could get a charter for a day or two. It sounded incredibly romantic to Fiona, and in the meantime, they had her room at the Byblos, which would be fun too. She felt as though she were dreaming every time she looked at him.

They walked around the Left Bank afterward, had a glass of wine on the terrace of the Deux Magots, and he bought her a silly little painting from a street artist, as a souvenir of their first days together in Paris. And at midnight they went back to the hotel, nearly raced to her room, and made love for hours. So much so that she overslept in the morning, and didn't wake until Adrian pounded on her door to say goodbye. He was leaving for the airport. His work in Paris was done.

'I thought you were supposed to be working,' he said in an accusing tone, but she knew he didn't mean it.

'I am . . . I mean I will . . . I was exhausted,' she apologized.

'So am I. I've been working my ass off since six, and you're still sleeping at ten-thirty. When I grow up, I want your job.' As he said it, he saw a pair of men's shoes, neatly sitting under the coffee table, and Adrian beamed at her. 'Unless your feet have grown, or you're cross-dressing, I assume that means you're no longer a virgin.'

'Mind your own business,' she said softly. She had closed the door to the bedroom, and John was still asleep. They hadn't gone to sleep until four in the morning, but it had been well worth it.

'How much will you give me not to tell Sir Winston?' Adrian said conspiratorially.

'My entire fortune.'

'*And* your turquoise bracelet? I can have it remade to fit me,' he said wickedly.

'The hell you will. Go ahead and tell him.'

'I may just have to do that. Are you still going to St. Tropez?' He had never seen her look like that, and he absolutely loved it. All he wanted was for her to be happy. He had liked John since the moment he met him. He thought he was terrific for her. As far as he was concerned, they were both lucky, and she deserved it. In all the years Adrian had known her, Fiona had never had a man in her life he approved of. Especially not the married architect from London. Adrian had loathed him. And he thought the conductor who wanted to marry her was silly. John was the only man he'd ever seen her with who he thought was worthy of her.

'Yes, I'm still going to St. Tropez,' she said innocently, but Adrian knew her better.

'Is he going with you?'

'Uh-huh,' she said, grinning mischievously.

'You naughty children! Well, enjoy it,' he said, hugging her. 'Call me if you need to tell me anything, and FedEx me everything before you leave.' She had a lot of work to do that day before she started her vacation, and she intended to do it. In love or not, Fiona was a woman who met her deadlines. And nothing was going to change that.

'I promise. Fly safely . . . I love you,' she said, and hugged him again, and he left in a flourish of bags, and his straw hat, and red alligator briefcase to match his sandals.

'I love you too. Say hi to John for me. Tell him I'll handle Sir Winston.' And with a last wave, he disappeared into the elevator as she hung out the door of the suite, and then closed the door softly. She didn't want to wake John, but he was stirring anyway when she slipped back into bed beside him.

'Who was that?' he asked sleepily, throwing an arm around her, and turning toward her. She loved the way he looked in the morning.

'Adrian. He just left. He tried to blackmail me, and said he's going to tell Sir Winston. He wants my turquoise bracelet. I told him to forget it.'

'He knows?' John opened an eye and looked at her cautiously. 'You told him?'

'He saw your shoes under the table.'

'Oh. How much does he want not to tell the dog?'

'He's not a dog.'

'Sorry, I forgot . . . Come here, you gorgeous thing, you . . .' he said, pulling her closer, and the day began as the night before had ended.

7

Fiona got all her work done and sent it to Adrian before they left for St. Tropez, and John managed to find a hundred-and-forty-foot sailboat for them to charter. The broker had promised she was a beauty, and they departed for St. Tropez in high spirits. John had left a message for both his girls that he was staying in France for another two weeks, but both had been out when he called them.

As soon as they got to Nice, Fiona had a limousine waiting for them to drive them to St. Tropez and the Hotel Byblos. She had an adorable suite there. The boat was meeting them the next morning.

They spent an hour on the beach that afternoon, and then wandered through the shops, and stopped at a café. That night, she took him to her favorite bistro. It was as noisy and crowded as she had warned him it would be, and after walking for a while, they went back to the hotel, and were content to fall into bed in each other's arms. They fell asleep this time almost as soon as their heads hit the pillow. It had been a long week, full of passion, people, and excitement, and they were both thrilled to be on vacation alone.

The next morning when they saw the boat, they were both awestruck by her beauty. They spent the day sailing her with a crew of nine, spent the night in the port in Monte Carlo, and had a quiet romantic dinner on the aft deck, drinking champagne and reveling in the joy of being together in glorious surroundings.

'How did this happen?' Fiona asked him in amazement. 'Did I miss something? When did I die and go to heaven? How did I get this lucky?' She had never even dreamed of finding anyone like him. And he felt exactly as she did. Fiona was magic.

'Maybe we both deserve this,' he said simply, and believed it.

'That's too simple. I feel like I won the lottery.'

'We both did,' he corrected.

For the next two weeks their time together was idyllic, beyond hopes and dreams and wishes.

They had the boat only for the first week, and made good use of it, and their time together after that was a little more prosaic. But they enjoyed that too, and had a good time in St. Tropez going to the beach and trying out new restaurants. The vacation ended all too quickly. It seemed like only minutes later that they were back in the airport in Nice, flying to Paris, and then flying home to New York together. For once,

Fiona wasn't even excited about seeing Sir Winston. And on the flight home, they discussed how to handle the rest of the summer.

John had already explained that his girls were away until Labor Day, his housekeeper was off visiting family, and his dog was at the kennel for the summer. She needed a lot of attention, and he couldn't take care of her properly with his housekeeper in North Dakota. And after spending Labor Day weekend with him, both his girls were going back to college, although he saw them regularly throughout the school year. Courtenay came home often for weekends since she was only in Princeton. Hilary did her best to come home from Brown once a month, except when she had exams. He said she was a very serious student. She wanted to be an oceanographer, and was doing an internship that summer at a lab in Long Beach, California. John had said a million times that he was certain Fiona was going to love them. There was no question in his mind that they would fall in love with her, just as he had. That part was easy. He was a little less sure of Fiona's reaction to them, since she had never had children of her own. But they weren't babies, they were women. So Fiona should be perfectly at ease with them, he told himself, and he was sure they would become the best of friends. His girls needed adult female companionship, since both of them missed their mother so much. Fiona had already said that she was going to go shopping with them. She didn't know much about kids and young people, but shopping was one thing she was good at, and she thought it would be an easy way to get to know his girls.

'So what are we going to do when we go home?' Fiona asked as they sat in the first-class lounge at Charles de Gaulle, waiting for their flight to New York.

'About what? I was thinking that maybe we could find a house in the Hamptons to rent for the weekends.' There might be one available that no one wanted, and they both loved the beach and getting out of town. Failing that, he could always charter another boat, which appealed to both of them as well. The possibilities were infinite, but she had another plan in mind. They had gone straight from dating and first blush to wanting to be together all the time. He had already said as much to her himself in St. Tropez.

'Do you want to stay at my place with me until your housekeeper comes home?' Fiona asked. He had thought of it himself, but didn't want to be presumptuous and suggest it to her.

'How do you think Sir Winston would feel about it? Do you think we should ask him first?'

'Don't worry. I'll negotiate the deal with him. How do you feel about it?'

'I think it's an excellent idea. My place is hard to take care of without Mrs. Westerman. And I have no one else to do the cleaning. There's a service that comes in once a week, but that's about it. Your place runs a little more smoothly, with Jamal, and it's easier for you with the dog . . . sorry . . . your son, I mean, Sir Winston.'

'That's better,' she said with a grin. She liked the arrangement very much – and then suddenly thought of her closets in a panic. She didn't have an inch of spare closet space, and she was going to have to find some for him fast. She was wondering if he would mind going down a flight of stairs to the guest room. She had her fur coats and ski clothes there, but she could probably squeeze out some space for him. Maybe. Or . . . maybe her office closet, but there was no hanging space . . . the bathroom closet . . . it was full of her night-gowns and robes and beach clothes, and some old evening gowns. She'd have to work out some-thing. He was a consummate good sport. He had been on the trip, whenever anything went wrong, although very little had. But he was unfailingly polite and easygoing, and she loved that about him. He didn't seem to have a temper, and had a happy disposition.

They went straight to her house that night. Jamal had left it immaculate for her, and filled the house with flowers. And the refrigerator was full of everything she liked to eat. There was even a bottle of champagne, which she opened to share with John, and they toasted each other, standing in the living room. She had never been as happy in her life. Sir Winston was coming home the next day, she could hardly wait to see him.

117

The next morning John cooked breakfast for her. He made a cheese omelette and English muffins, and they left the house at the same time for their respective offices. Jamal arrived just as they went out, and he stared at Fiona in surprise. Men had spent the night from time to time over the years, and the conductor had lived with her, but he hadn't seen anyone at the house in the morning in a very long time. He didn't know if this was a temporary fling for her, or someone who was going to stick around. Her next words to him spelled it out.

'This is Mr. Anderson, Jamal. I need a key for him,' she said offhandedly, she had an important meeting at the office and was in a hurry. 'Just make a copy and leave it on my desk.' She reminded him that he had to be there when they brought Sir Winston home at four o'clock, and with that she and John hailed cabs simultaneously, kissed in the middle of the street, and left for their respective workdays.

They had promised to meet at her place that night. He was going to his apartment first to pick up some stuff. It was as easy as that. Presto magic, she was living with a man in her house. For the summer at least. Until his daughters and house-keeper came back. Once the girls left for school again, she assumed he would move back in with her again, as long as they both liked it. And she hoped they would. She hoped so with all her heart. She wanted this to work, more than she'd ever wanted anything in her life. She was seriously in love with him, and thought him an extraordinary man. And she knew he felt the same way about her. Blind luck.

'How was St. Tropez?' Adrian asked with a knowing grin as she came through the door with an armful of papers and files and magazines she'd brought back from Paris. They had a lot to talk about.

'Fabulous.' She beamed at him, he could see it in her eyes. She had never looked as relaxed.

'And where is he now?'

'At his office.'

'Where was he last night?' Adrian teased. He was like a brother to her, and she didn't mind. She had few secrets from him, if any.

'None of your business.'

'I thought so. Have you told Sir Winston yet?'

'We're breaking the news to him tonight.'

'Call the vet and get Valium for him. This could be hard.'

'I know.' And then she lowered her voice. 'I have a serious problem, and I don't know what to do about it.'

He looked instantly worried for her. 'Nothing too serious, I hope.'

'It could be. Adrian, I need closet space. I don't have room for so much as a hankie in my closets.'

'Is he moving in?' Adrian looked impressed. This was quick. But that's how things happened sometimes. And this had.

'Sort of. For the summer. Till his housekeeper gets back. I swear, if he brings over so much as a pair of pajamas, I'm screwed. I looked in every closet last night. My fur coats are in the guest room, my summer stuff's upstairs. My evening gowns, nightgowns, office clothes – hell, Adrian, I have more stuff than a store. I don't have room for a guy.'

'You'd better find some fast. Guys don't like digging their boxers out of your pantyhose drawer, or fighting through your evening gowns to dress for work. If he doesn't cross-dress, you have a serious problem.'

'He doesn't.'

'You're screwed. Sell your clothes.'

'Don't be ridiculous. You have to figure something out.'

'*I* have to figure something out? Do I look like the closet police? He's not moving in with me, he's moving in with you.'

'What would you do? You have as much junk as I do.'

'How about renting one of those nice trailers and parking it on the sidewalk for your clothes?' He was vastly amused by her dilemma, but they both knew it was a nice one to have.

'You're not funny.'

'No, but you are. Just toss all your stuff out of one closet, and maybe dump it in the guest room, or put it on rolling racks, and push it around the house.'

'Great idea.' She looked relieved. 'Do me a favor, go to Gracious Home at lunchtime and buy me a bunch of racks. Have someone take them to the house. I'll tell Jamal to set them up in the guest room, and I'll just empty a closet for him tonight.'

'Perfect. See, people make a huge mistake. They think the challenge in relationships comes from sex or money. That's absolutely not true. It comes from closets. I had to ask my last lover to move out. It was him or my Blahniks. I felt terrible about it, but in the end, I was more attached to my shoes.' She knew him better than that, and also knew that his last lover had cheated on him, and Adrian had been heartbroken and thrown him out and cried for weeks. He was a decent guy, and the boyfriend hadn't been. He had damn near broken Adrian's heart.

'You're a genius. Just get me the racks. I'll try and get home early and start emptying a closet for him. I feel so stupid to have so much stuff.'

'You'd feel dumber in our line of work if you were badly dressed. Let's be real here.'

'All right, so we're shallow, terribly spoiled people. And you're right. Maybe I'll rent an apartment for my clothes and just switch seasons. That way I'll only need half the closets.'

'See if the relationship works first. How is it, by the way? I assume it must be okay if you're letting him move in with you.'

'He's not moving in,' she corrected him. 'He is staying with me for the summer.'

'Sorry, "staying with you." Things must be pretty good. No one has "stayed with you" in years.' Adrian reminded her of what she knew already.

'I figured no one ever would again. I thought it was me and Sir Winston for eternity, or as long as we both shall live.'

'One of you is going to live longer than the other in that relationship. And considering Sir Winston's age and heart problems, I hope it's you.' She nodded, sobered by the comment. She liked to believe that Sir Winston would live forever. Adrian figured she'd be lucky if she got another year or two out of him, if that. He had already had a couple of close calls. He just hoped, for Fiona's sake, that sharing her with a two-legged admirer wouldn't push Sir Winston over the edge.

Having solved her most pressing problems of the hour, Adrian and Fiona got to work. He brought her up to date on all the follow-up from Paris. She had a general staff meeting set for eleven o'clock, which, as it turned out, went till two. She spent the rest of the afternoon catching up, looking at shots of the couture, and checking on schedules and details for shoots. They were insanely busy. They had just closed October and were starting on November. And in another month they were going to be up to their ears in Christmas, which was always a big issue. And Fiona was disappointed to discover that two of her favorite junior editors had quit while she was away and had already left. Adrian had hired replacements for them while she was gone.

She was startled to realize there was a major shoot scheduled for later that week with Brigitte Lacombe. And an even more complicated one with Mario Testino over the weekend. It was going to be a totally insane week. Welcome home.

But in spite of everything happening, she managed to leave the office by six o'clock and almost flew home. Adrian had sent someone out for the racks for her, and Jamal had set them up in the guest room, although she didn't discover until they collapsed twice with all her evening gowns on them that he had set them up wrong. He had been holding the diagram upside down. And he helped her get them right.

'You must really like this guy,' Jamal commented, as she picked all her evening gowns up off the floor for the third time and put them on the rack. She had taken all of two minutes to kiss and hug Sir Winston, and he had given her the cold shoulder. He did not like going to 'camp,' and whenever he did, he took it out on her for weeks afterward. She was in the doghouse. And he was stretched out on her bed, snoring loudly.

'He's a great guy,' she said about John, as she added some of her beach clothes to the rack, and about a dozen nightgowns. By the time she was through, she had made space in about a third of one closet for him to hang suits, and there was room for about four or five pairs of shoes on the floor. And she had freed up two drawers. It didn't look like much, but it had taken her two hours to do it. John had called at seven and explained that he had gotten held up at the office, he hadn't gotten to the apartment yet, and hoped to be home by nine. And if she wanted him to, he would bring pizza and wine. She said it was okay, she would make them a salad and an omelette, which he said sounded good to him. She smiled to herself as she hung up, it felt wonderful being domestic with him.

Jamal had left by then, and she scouted through her closets again, looking for things to remove. She finally managed to part with a couple of ski parkas she rarely used, and the big down coat she wore when it snowed. They took up a lot of room, but translated into closet space, she suspected it would give him room for only two or three more suits. Closet space seemed to be harder to find than gold. And she would rather dig the gold out of her teeth than give up a whole closet to him. That was asking a lot, no matter how much she loved him.

She sat down on the bed next to Sir Winston then, and he looked at her, moaned, and turned around with his back to her. She got the point and went to take a shower before John got home. Everything was different suddenly. Now, instead of lying on the bed at night, looking a mess, and eating tuna fish out of a can, or eating a banana and a rice cake, she had to look decent, maybe even sexy and glamorous, and provide a meal for both of them. But it was fun. And it was only for the summer. It was like playing house. She put on a pale pink silk caftan and gold sandals, and she set the table and made salad. She was planning to do the omelette when he got home.

When he did, at nearly ten o'clock finally, he looked exhausted. Worse than she had when she got home. He was carrying armloads of clothes, which he dragged out of a cab, with two shopping bags full of belts, ties, underwear, and socks. He looked as if he were moving in, and for a fraction of a second, her heart gave a flutter. And then she instantly remembered how lucky she was and how much she loved him. When he kissed her, it reminded her, and he dropped all his belongings on the floor of the front hall. After he kissed her, he looked around expectantly and asked, 'Where's the dog? . . . sorry . . . the boy . . . the man . . . your friend . . . you know, Sir Winston?' He had to remember to get it right. Every time he said the d-word, she looked like she'd been slapped. She was a little sensitive on the subject – and apparently, so was the dog.

'He's mad at me. He went to bed.'

'Our bed? . . . Your bed?' She nodded, and he smiled and kissed her again. He was a good sport, but it was after all Sir Winston's house. He got there first.

'You must be starving. I made a salad. Do you want an omelette now?'

'To be honest, I'm not even hungry. I made a

cup of soup at the apartment. Mrs. Westerman left all the cupboards empty. It looks like no one lives there.'

'No one does for now.' Fiona smiled proudly, thinking of the closet space she had cleared for him. She hoped he would be pleased.

'You know what I'd love, I'd love to take a shower and just relax. You don't have to cook anything for me.' She wasn't hungry either, so she put the place mats and cutlery away and left the salad in the fridge. She grabbed a banana and helped him carry his things upstairs. He had also brought his shoeshine kit, and his Water Pik. He was diligent about his teeth and flossed for ages at night.

When they got upstairs, they dumped all his clothes on the bed. It was only when she heard the snoring underneath them that she realized they had covered Sir Winston, and she quickly took them off. He raised his head, glared at them, laid his head down again, and snored louder. He sounded like a power drill as he droned on, and Fiona smiled.

'Does that mean he approves, or not?' John asked, looking down at him in bemusement. He had never heard anything but a machine sound like that. 'Did you tell him about us?'

'More or less. I think we just did.'

'What did he say?'

'Not much.'

'Good,' he said, looking relieved. He was too

tired to negotiate with a dog. It had been a hellish day, and they had new problems on two accounts. Nothing insoluble, but it had eaten up his day and worn him out. He was dead, and all he wanted was a shower and bed. He walked into the bathroom, while Fiona hung up his clothes, and when he came back out twenty minutes later, he felt human again, and clean, and all his things were put away.

Fiona showed him his two drawers. He felt like a kid at camp, or his first day in boarding school, learning where his locker was. Everything was unfamiliar here, but he didn't mind. All he wanted was to be with her. And then she showed him where she had hung his suits and shirts. They were nicely squeezed in to the left of hers, without a centimeter of spare room, but they fit. He stared at them for a moment, wondering why she hadn't made more room, but decided not to say anything. There was some sort of gown with feathers on it draped over one of his dark suits.

'Not a lot of room, is there,' he commented, and she hated to admit it, but the closet seemed to have shrunk since that afternoon. She had been so proud of the space she'd made for him, and now it didn't seem like enough. She promised herself to study the problem again the next day. She needed more racks. But John was too tired to care. He turned on the TV, and lay on the bed, as Sir Winston lifted his head, looked at him in despair, and appeared to collapse deeper into the bed. But at least he didn't growl. John wasn't sure he could sleep with the noise he made, but he was willing to try, and he was so tired that night, it actually didn't bother him. He fell asleep with the television on, and Fiona in his arms. That was all he wanted. And when he awoke the next morning, Fiona had orange juice and coffee waiting for him, handed him the newspaper, and made him scrambled eggs. The dog was already outside.

All was well in their little world. Their first night had gone well. Fiona was enormously relieved as she left for work. And John sent her roses that afternoon. Adrian raised an eyebrow when he saw them on her desk.

'The dog didn't drive him insane?'

'Apparently not. We slept like triplets in the womb. And I made him breakfast this morning,' she said proudly.

'When was the last time you did that?'

'On Mother's Day when I was twelve.' Adrian knew she hated doing anything other than dressing and leaving for work in the morning.

'Sweet Jesus,' Adrian said, rolling his eyes toward heaven, looking like a boy at a revival meeting, 'it must be love!'

8

John proved to be as remarkable as Fiona hoped he would be. He was even understanding about it when she told him she had to stay in town and work her first weekend home. She had the Testino shoot to oversee, and she absolutely had to be there. John said he had plenty of work to do, and he even dropped by the shoot to see how it was going. He found it fascinating, and he cooked dinner for her when she got home. It was well over a hundred degrees, and she had been standing on the sidewalk in the blazing heat all day. And after they took a bath together, he gave her a massage.

'How did I ever get this lucky?' she said with a happy groan as he kneaded her aching back.

'We're both lucky,' he said happily. He was so pleased to be living with her, and to have companionship again. He enjoyed the slightly zany aspects of her life. It was all new to him. 'I took Sir Winston for a walk tonight, after it cooled off,' he said quietly. 'We had a long talk. He said he forgives me for the intrusion. Apparently, the only thing that bothers him is that he's afraid I'm going to take over his closet.' He was razzing her, and she moaned. She hadn't had a minute to do anything about it all week. John had pointed out to her that his suits were crushed, and he had to press a shirt himself one morning before work. His clothes were being devoured by hers.

'I'm sorry. I totally forgot. I swear, I'll take more stuff out of my closet tomorrow.' But the racks in the guest room were already full. She was going to have to dump her things on the bed. It was a small price to pay. And the following day, true to her word, she did. She took out all her leather skirts and pants, and laid them gingerly on the guest room bed. It at least gave him room for some more suits and shirts. He seemed to have a lot. She was just glad it wasn't winter. There would have been absolutely no room at all for his coats.

The following weekend they went out to the Hamptons, and much to her delight, for the entire month of August, he chartered a boat. It wasn't as big as the one they'd had in St. Tropez, but it was a beautiful sailboat nonetheless, and they had a great time with it. Adrian even sailed on it with them one weekend. And between the boat, their work, and meeting a few of each other's friends, the summer seemed to speed by, and was a great success. Sir Winston got used to John. Jamal said he was a true gentleman, and by the end of August, Fiona had conceded nearly half a closet. By then they were working on the December issue,

130

and the entire office seemed to be nuts. It was that time of year. Christmas in August for her.

And as planned months before, John left to meet his daughters in San Francisco for the Labor Day weekend. Hilary had finished her internship by then, and Courtenay had successfully completed her job at camp. John had told Fiona that he was going to tell the girls about her over the weekend. Their mother had been gone for more than two years, and John had no doubt that the girls would be happy for him. Both Mrs. Westerman and his dog were due home over the weekend. The summer was over. The dog had actually been Ann's. Fiona had fantasies about the two dogs meeting, and falling instantly in love. And she was both nervous and excited about meeting the girls. She had volunteered to pick them all up at the airport on Monday night. John thought it a terrific plan.

He wanted the four of them to have dinner that week, so Fiona could get to know the girls before they went back to college. They were going to be in town for only a few days. And after that he and Fiona had to figure out what they were going to do about their living arrangements. She didn't really have room for him, although he was happy staying with her, but her closets were a nightmare, and she couldn't seem to find space for him. But he also felt a little odd bringing her into the apartment where he had lived with Ann. And he wasn't sure how the girls would feel about it either. It still seemed a little delicate to him. And Fiona said it made her feel odd as well. They hadn't figured that out yet, and they had talked about the possibility of commuting between their two homes, although it created a problem for Fiona with her dog. She didn't want to uproot him, nor leave him alone all night at her house. Sooner or later she knew they would figure it out.

The main thing was that they were happy and got along, better than she ever had with anyone. Adrian was thrilled for them. And in the end, Fiona decided to spend the Labor Day weekend in town, instead of going to Martha's Vineyard, as she did every year. They had been away every weekend, and with John in California for the weekend, she had some things she wanted to fix and put away at her house. She had been relentlessly busy all month, and it was going to be nice to just stay home and chill out. She and Adrian went to a movie one night. And the next night she took her old mentor to dinner. It was nice to have some free time on her hands. She had less of it now that she was unofficially living with John. They were together all the time, and kept to themselves like two lovebirds. Even Adrian complained he never saw her anymore. But it was to be expected now that she was living with a man. How times had changed.

Her first indication that things were not going entirely according to plan in San Francisco was when John called, sounding somewhat nervous, and told her that she didn't need to pick them up at the airport. They would just take a cab home, and he would see her the next day.

'Is something wrong?' she asked, with a rock in her stomach. Her instinct told her that it was.

'Not at all,' he said calmly. 'The girls just want a little more time with their dad, and they'll be tired after the flight. They both want to meet you when they're fresh.' Fresh? It seemed an odd choice of words, they weren't flying in from Tokyo after all, but Fiona didn't argue with him. She mentioned it to Adrian when she saw him for brunch the next day. They sat in her garden going over layouts, and she mentioned the conversation to him.

'They probably didn't expect him to find a serious partner so soon. Neither did I.' Adrian smiled at her.

'*Soon?* I haven't had a date in two years,' Fiona exclaimed with feeling.

'I know. I know. I think we all just expect our friends to hang around forever, with nothing else to do. It's always a shock when they find someone and disappear.'

'I haven't disappeared,' she reassured him, and gave him a hug.

'I know that. But his kids may not be as mature as I am. Besides, you're a woman, so they might see you as a threat. And it confirms to them that their mother's gone for good. People have denial about things like that, especially kids.'

'How do you know so much?' She could see his point.

'I don't. I'm just guessing. See what he says when he comes back.'

But when she met John on Tuesday morning for breakfast, he didn't say much. And he looked strained. She asked him how the trip was and he said, 'Great,' but she wasn't convinced. He kissed her, but he didn't even look happy to see her. More than anything, he looked nervous and stressed. He said that he wanted her to come to the apartment for dinner. He was staying there that week, and the girls were going back to college over the weekend. He was driving Courtenay to Princeton on Saturday, and setting her up in the dorm. Hilary was moving into a house with friends.

'And how is Mrs. Westerman?' Fiona asked benignly, and John glanced at her with a look of terror when she asked.

'She's fine,' he said vaguely, and changed the subject, and when Fiona got to the office, she looked scared when she saw her friend.

'Something's wrong,' she said to Adrian. 'I think he fell out of love with me over the weekend. He looks crazed.'

'Maybe something happened with his kids. Give him a chance, Fiona. He'll tell you about it when things calm down. Is he moving back in with you after they go back to school?'

'He didn't say.' She was nearly panicked, but

trying to stay calm. But she had never seen him as weird as he was that day.

'You'd better start clearing out your closets. You don't want him getting comfortable at home again. Or do you?' Adrian asked pointedly, and she shook her head, looking grief-stricken. She was terrified that she had already lost him, but it couldn't have happened that fast. It didn't make sense to her.

'No, I don't,' she answered. 'I want him to come back.'

'Then just relax, and give him space. He'll be okay. He loves you, Fiona. That doesn't change overnight.'

'He fell in love with me overnight, maybe he'll fall out of love with me just as fast.'

'You have to adjust and compromise. You both need time to grow into this. Besides, you two have been living in never-never land all summer. Now his kids are back. You're in real time. You have to adapt to that, at least until the kids leave again. See how it goes.'

'I'm having dinner with them tonight,' Fiona said, sounding terrified. He had never seen her look like that in all the years they had been friends. Fiona was never afraid of anything, and surely not two young girls. She had never even been afraid of men. But that was also because she never cared if she lost them. Until now, she had always been just as happy to be alone. Until John. Now she cared. And she had more to lose.

135

'What time are you meeting them?'

'Seven-thirty. At his place. His housekeeper is cooking dinner. I've never been to his apartment. He hasn't gone back all summer, except to pick up clothes, and I never bothered to go with him. But he didn't invite me to either. Now I wish I'd gone. New place. New people. New ball game. Shit, Adrian, I'm scared.'

'Relax. You'll be fine.' He couldn't believe it. The woman who terrified half the magazine industry, if not all of it, was scared witless of a housekeeper and two girls.

'I've never even seen his dog.'

'For chrissake, Fiona, if he can put up with yours, you ought to be able to make friends with a pit bull. Give them all a chance. Take a Valium or something. You'll be fine.'

They never had a chance to talk about it again for the rest of the afternoon. They were insanely busy, had endless meetings, and a thousand unexpected crises and problems cropped up. At least she spoke to John twice between meetings, and he sounded more normal again. She admitted to him that she was nervous about dinner, and he reassured her and told her he loved her. After that, she was less worried. It was just the newness of it all, and she had never had to meet anyone's kids, nor cared so much. She was sitting in a meeting with Adrian and four other editors at the end of the day, when he suddenly looked at her. And this time he looked panicked as he glanced at his watch.

'What time are you supposed to be there?'

'Seven-thirty. Why?' Fiona looked blank, with three pencils stuck in her hair.

'It's ten after eight. Get your ass out of here.'

'Oh, shit!' She looked as panicked as he did, as the other editors watched them, not knowing what it was about. 'I wanted to go home and change.'

'Forget it. Wash your face, and put on lipstick in the cab. You look fine. Go! Go!' He shooed her out of the meeting, and she left at a dead run, apologizing vaguely, and called John on her cell phone from a cab. It was eight twenty-five by then. She was nearly an hour late, and she apologized profusely, and said she had lost track of the time in a meeting about a serious crisis that had come up about the December issue. He told her not to worry about it, but he sounded strained and annoyed. And when she got to the apartment, she saw why.

The apartment itself was large and handsomely decorated, but everything about it seemed cold and uptight. And on literally every surface there were framed photographs of his late wife. The living room looked like a shrine to her, and there was an enormous portrait of her on one wall, and on either side of it were portraits of the two girls. They had had them done just before she died. She was a pretty woman, and she had the look of a debutante who had grown up to be head of the Junior League. Even in the photographs it was easy to see that she had none of Fiona's panache and style, nor was she as beautiful. But she had the saintly look of the perfect wife. She was the kind of woman who normally bored Fiona to tears, but she instantly forced those thoughts from her mind, and entered the apartment apologizing profusely, and explaining about the meeting again. She was nearly in tears. John kissed her gently on the cheek and gave her a hug.

'It's okay,' he whispered, 'I understand. The girls are just a little upset about their mother.'

'Why?' Fiona looked blank. Her mind wasn't working, she was too upset about being late to understand what he was saying. Why were they upset about their mother? She had been dead for two years.

'Because they think my being with you is a betrayal of her,' John explained hurriedly before they entered the living room. 'They feel like I didn't love her, because I want to be with someone else.'

'She's been gone for two years,' Fiona whispered back.

'I know. They need time to adjust.' And she was an hour late. That didn't help. She felt sorry for him suddenly. He looked like he'd had a rough few days. And he had.

As Fiona walked across the living room, she saw two stern looking young women sitting rigidly on the couch. They looked as though they had been forced there at gunpoint, and they nearly had.

She'd seen happier-looking people in hostage situations, and they glared at her without remorse. Neither of them said a word.

Fiona walked over to the older-looking one of the two, who she assumed was Hilary, and stuck out her hand. 'Hello, Hilary, I'm Fiona. It's nice to meet you,' she said politely, trying to sound both warm and unthreatening. And the girl glared at her and did not extend her hand.

'I'm Courtenay. And I think what you're both doing is disgusting.' It was certainly one way to start a conversation. Fiona didn't know what to say in response, and was frozen on the spot, while John looked as though he were about to faint or throw up.

'I'm sorry you feel that way,' Fiona said calmly, finding her tongue finally. 'I understand. This must be hard for both of you. But I'm not trying to take your father away from you. We just like spending time together. He's not going anywhere.'

'That's not true. He already has. He's been living with you all summer. The doorman said he only came here to pick up clothes.' Fiona learned later that Mrs. Westerman had checked, and told the girls. The little dear.

'We spent some time together, and he's probably lonely here without you,' Fiona said, glancing at the other sister then. John looked crushed by the exchange, and as if he were about to burst into tears. He hadn't expected this reaction from his children, he was sorely disappointed in them, and deeply hurt. He had been loyal and faithful to their mother and her memory, he had done everything he could to save her, and stood by her till the end. And he had been there for his daughters, without reservation, ever since. Now they were begrudging him any kind of happiness with another woman, and had vowed to hate Fiona on sight, which they did. Beyond reason. 'It's nice to meet you, Hilary,' Fiona continued, as she stood awkwardly in their living room, and no one asked her to sit down. John was standing next to her, looking devastated. He'd been going through this since San Francisco, and it had been totally unexpected. And relentless. He had no idea what to do with them, or how to turn it around. He was mortified that they had been rude to Fiona. He had told them that he expected them to at least be polite. He had also told them that Fiona was a wonderful woman, and it wasn't her fault that their mother had died. Nor his. But they had said they hated him and Fiona anyway, and cried all weekend. And so had he. Now he was running out of patience, and getting angry at them for being so unreasonable. Hilary was ignoring Fiona entirely. She was the prettier of the two, although they were almost identical and looked like twins. Both were blue-eyed blondes like their mother, but they had a look of John about them too.

'You both seem to have forgotten your manners,' he said sternly. 'There's no reason to punish Fiona for going out with me. I've been faithful to your mother's memory for two years. Fiona has nothing to do with this. She's a free woman and she has every right to go out with me, and I have every right to be with her, if I choose.'

But before either of them could comment, a stern, spare, angry-looking older woman walked into the living room. She was wearing a navy dress with an apron over it, sensible black orthopedic shoes, and her hair was pulled back so tightly in a bun, she nearly looked like Olive Oyl, with none of the charm. She looked like an angry cartoon. Fiona had to fight an overwhelming urge to say 'Mrs. Westerman, I presume,' but fortunately she didn't. Instead, John made the introduction for her, and Mrs. Westerman refused to acknowledge her, she just looked straight at him.

'Dinner's been ready for an hour and a half. Are you going to eat?' she said sternly to him. It was nine o'clock by then, and Fiona apologized to her as well for being late, and the older woman refused to even look at her, as she turned on her heel and stomped back into the kitchen. She clearly was on the side of the two girls, and the late Mrs. Anderson. Fiona couldn't help wondering if John's late wife would have been this unreasonable. It was hard to believe the level of hostility she was getting from them, harder still to understand.

John waited for the girls to stand up, and followed them into the dining room. It was definitely not going to be an easy dinner, and

Fiona felt desperately sorry for him. He was doing all he could to keep the ship afloat. But she felt as though they were having dinner on the *Titanic*, and were going down fast.

The girls took their places, as John motioned Fiona to a seat next to him, with a look of grief-stricken apology, and she smiled at him to reassure him. Somehow she knew they were going to get through it, whatever it took, and afterward they could talk about it with compassion and humor. She was determined to be there for him, and was trying to give him all the strength she could. And as she looked at him lovingly, Mrs. Westerman walked into the dining room and slammed dinner on the table. The roast beef was dry and charred beyond all recognition, and the potatoes around it had been burned to a crisp. The vegetable, whatever it had once been, was unrecognizable, and literally nothing on the table was edible. Instead of slowing dinner down when Fiona was late, or taking things off the stove, Mrs. Westerman had just let everything keep cooking, to prove the point, and register her own disapproval of her employer's alleged treason. She had pledged her allegiance to the girls when they came home from San Francisco the night before and told her what had happened over the summer while they were all gone, and she was outraged and said that everything their father was doing, whatever it was, was a sin. And she didn't want to work for a sinner. She had told the girls she might quit over it, which

142

had frightened them even more. She had told John the same thing when he got home from the office that night. Like the girls, she was punishing him.

Fiona knew she had been with the family since Hilary was born, twenty-one years, and she was going to do everything she could to make life difficult for him. It was not only unfair, it was sick.

'What do you say we order a pizza?' Fiona said, trying to lighten the mood, but both girls glared at her, as Mrs. Westerman slammed a door in the kitchen, and could be heard banging cupboards loudly throughout the meal.

'I'm not hungry anyway,' Hilary said, and stood up, as Courtenay instantly followed suit. Without another word to their father, or her, both girls marched to their rooms. Fiona sat and looked at John sympathetically, and reached out to touch his hand, but he looked as though he had been beaten, and could barely look at her. He was not only heartbroken at the way they had treated him, but deeply ashamed at having exposed Fiona to that scene.

'I'm so sorry, sweetheart,' Fiona said to him.

'So am I,' he said in a hoarse voice, rough with tears. 'I can't believe they behaved that way, and I'm sorry about dinner too. Mrs. Westerman was extremely loyal to Ann, which was wonderful, but that's no reason to do this to you. I'm sorry I put you through it.'

'I'm sorry I was late. That didn't make things any easier. I totally lost track of time.'

'It wouldn't have made any difference. They've been like this since I told them on Saturday. I thought they would be so happy for us, and for me. I was shocked, and I thought they'd get over it by the next day, but they didn't, they just got worse.' She was suddenly afraid that it might mean the end of the relationship, she looked frightened when she looked at him, and he saw it too. He was a decent man, and his heart went out to her. He got up from where he was sitting, and went to put his arms around her to reassure her, just as Mrs. Westerman opened the kitchen door, and let Fifi, the family Pekingese, into the room. She had been the late Mrs. Anderson's beloved pet, and had been Mrs. Westerman's charge ever since. Fifi paused in the doorway, growling as she looked at them, and seeing Fiona and John with their arms around each other, it was hard to say if she thought Fiona was attacking him, but without pausing for breath, she flew straight out of the kitchen like a heat-seeking missile, and landed at Fiona's feet. And before either of them knew what had happened, she had sunk her teeth with full force into Fiona's ankle. It had surprised her more than anything, but the dog absolutely refused to let go, as Fiona clutched John, and he poured a pitcher of water onto the dog, and then yanked her away from Fiona and threw her toward the kitchen. The dog left yelping, and soaked, as Mrs. Westerman screamed that he had tried to kill the dog, and ran shrieking into the kitchen in tears

144

with the dog in her arms, and no apology to Fiona, who was bleeding profusely from a nasty little wound.

John put a wet napkin on it, and sat her down. Fiona was shaking, and felt utterly ridiculous for the mess she was making. But her ankle wouldn't stop bleeding, as John put pressure on the wound, and then looked at her miserably as he helped her hobble into the kitchen, and shouted a warning to Mrs. Westerman to lock up the dog. But she had already retreated to her room with Fifi. They could hear the dog barking furiously through the door. All John wanted to do was get the hell out, and go home with Fiona, but he knew he had to stay till the girls went back to school at least. He had never been through anything like this. He studied her ankle, as she sat on the kitchen counter, with her foot in the sink, and he looked at her with embarrassment and grief.

'I hate to say it, Fiona, but I think you need stitches.'

'Don't worry about it,' she said calmly, wanting to make the horror of the evening better for him, 'these things happen.'

'Only in horror movies,' he said grimly. He tied a kitchen towel around her leg, helped her off the counter, and walked her out of the apartment gingerly, as they both watched the blood stain the towel quickly. It had already soaked through by the time they hailed a cab, and blood was dripping down her foot as John carried her into the hospital and deposited her in the emergency room with a look of disbelief.

When the doctor on duty examined her finally, he said it was a deep wound, and she needed stitches. He administered a local anesthetic and sewed her up, gave her a tetanus shot, since she hadn't had one in years, and then gave her antibiotics and painkillers to take home with her. She was looking a little green around the gills by then. She hadn't eaten since breakfast, and it had been a rough evening. She got dizzy on the way out, and had to sit down for a minute.

'I'm sorry I'm such a wimp,' she apologized, 'it's really nothing.' She tried to make light of it for him, but she was feeling awful. The anesthetic was wearing off, her ankle was killing her, and the little beast had bitten as hard as it could, nearly as hard as his daughters. The dog was their alter ego – and Mrs. Westerman's as well.

'Nothing? My daughters were horrible, the housekeeper was unthinkable, and my dog attacked you, and you just had eight stitches and a tetanus shot. What the hell do you mean, nothing?' He was furious, and didn't know who to take it out on. 'I'm taking you home,' he said miserably, and told her to stay where she was till he found a cab. He was back five minutes later, and carried her out, and when he got her home, he undressed her, put her to bed, gave her her medicine, and propped her foot up on a pillow. He went downstairs to get them both something to eat and make her a cup of tea, and when he came upstairs with a tray, she already looked better, and he made a decision. He told her he had, and she looked terrified as she waited to hear it. After a night like that, he could only have come to a single conclusion, that having Fiona in his life was just too difficult for him. She sat stoically while he gathered his thoughts and looked at the woman he had fallen in love with in Paris, or even before that. It had been love at first sight for him.

'Fiona, if you'll have me, I'd like to move in with you this weekend, after I take Courtenay back to Princeton. Hilary is leaving Friday night for Brown. I'm not staying in the apartment with that woman. There's no reason for me to be there. I want to be here with you.' He looked down at the sleeping bulldog, who had barely stirred when they got home, and smiled. 'And Sir Winston. The girls will just have to get used to it. I'll go home when they come for holidays or weekends. And eventually, I hope you'll come with me. We'll get you shin guards and a stun gun to use on Mrs. Westerman and the dog. Will you have me?' he asked almost humbly, and she burst into tears. She had been so sure he was about to tell her it was over, and she didn't want to lose him. She was just so sorry that his daughters hated her. The house-keeper was another story, and the dog was a little beast. But she was truly upset about his children.

'Are you sure you want to do that?' she asked, looking worried.

147

'Yes, I am,' he said firmly. He had no qualms about it. And he had never been as angry at his children, or as disappointed.

She couldn't stop crying as she looked at him, and he took her in his arms again. She had had a hell of an evening. 'I'd love you to move in with me,' she said, still unable to stop crying as he held her. It was as much the shock of what had happened as the relief that he didn't want to leave her.

'Then why are you crying?' he said gently.

'Because I'll have to make more room in my closets,' she said, and laughed through her tears, and he joined her.

9

Fiona was sitting at her desk the next day when Adrian came in to see her, after a meeting. She was looking at photographs on a light box behind her desk, and swiveled around as he came in.

'So how was it?' He had been dying of curiosity all night, and hadn't had time to stop in to see her all morning, and the one time he did, there were people with her.

'It was interesting,' she said obliquely.

'What does that mean?'

'Well, the housekeeper hated me and probably tried to poison me, but she burned the dinner so totally that I never got to eat it. The girls said they hated me, and haven't spoken to their father since Saturday when he told them. They refused to talk to me, told us we were disgusting, and stomped off to their rooms since there was nothing to eat anyway. And then the dog attacked me.' But at least she smiled at him when she said it. She hadn't lost her sense of humor.

'You're exaggerating, I hope. About the dog at

least. Seriously, how bad was it? Did the kids lighten up eventually?'

'No. And I wasn't kidding about the dog either. I had eight stitches.'

'Are you serious?' He looked thunderstruck, and with that she lifted her leg onto the desk and rested it there, it was heavily bandaged and an impressive sight.

'I had a tetanus shot, and I'm on antibiotics. The only good news is that he was so upset, I thought he was going to end it with me. Instead, he's moving in this weekend.' She looked delighted as Adrian stared at her leg in disbelief.

'Oh God, what are you going to do about your closets?'

'I'll have to figure out something. Maybe I'll turn the dining room into a giant closet. Or tent the garden. God knows, but I'll have to do something. At least he still wants me. Jesus, Adrian. The kids were beyond awful. They were monsters, to him mostly, but they were awful to me too. And the housekeeper is right out of *Rebecca*, or some equally scary movie. I thought she was going to kill me. Instead, she had the dog do it. Thank God they don't have a pit bull.'

'What was it?' He looked worried. Even with her amusing recital of it, it was a pretty ugly story. And his daughters sounded like real bitches.

'A Pekingese, thank God. The damn thing wouldn't get its teeth out of my leg. John had to pour water on it.'

'Holy shit, Fiona, this is awful!' He was laughing because she made it sound so funny, but she had been scared.

'It was pretty bad,' she admitted ruefully. 'I guess I won't be going there for Thanksgiving.'

'You can have turkey with me. My dogs love you.' He had two beautiful Hungarian sheepdogs, and they adored her. They nearly killed her with kisses whenever they saw her.

'I don't know what John is going to do. Maybe time will take care of it. His daughters are really going to be a problem. Or at least they are for the moment. They think he's betraying the memory of their mother.'

'That's ridiculous. You said she's been gone for two years. What do they expect? He's a young man. He can't bury himself with her.'

'I know. But they don't see it that way. I guess they want him to themselves, but they're not even there. They're away at college.'

'They'll get over it. At least he's not letting it sway him, or turn him against you.'

'On the contrary, when we got back from the hospital, he told me he wanted to move in with me. And that's a little scary too. That's pretty quick. We've only been together for two and a half months. I would have waited a lot longer, but on the other hand I like living with him. And I've gotten used to him. I missed him all weekend.'

'Can he stand your crazy life? Jamal, the dog, the groupies, me, all the people who hang around you, the shoots till all hours, the deadlines, all the nutcases you collect? He seems pretty conservative. Make sure you give him space and don't drive him crazy. You can't live like you did when you were alone, Fiona. You're going to have to make adjustments for him, especially if he's really living with you and not just "staying with you," as you put it.'

'He's held up so far. And he's not giving up his apartment, he can always stay there for a day or two for a breather, if he needs one,' she said practically, but Adrian shook his head in disapproval.

'Don't push him till he needs a breather. I know how you are. You like doing things your way. It's your house and your life and your dog. I'm the same way, and I've made the same mistake in every relationship I've had. I forget to compromise and adjust, and sooner or later it drives them right out the door. You'd better think about it, Fiona.' It was a sobering warning, and she suspected he was right.

'I know, I know,' she said with a smile. 'It's hard to do sometimes. I'm set in my ways.'

'That's no excuse. We can all make adjustments. And it would be stupid to lose him. I think this time it would really matter to you.' He was right, and she knew it.

'Yes, it would. I don't want to lose him. But I sure don't know what to do about his daughters.'

'Let him handle it. They're his problem. You're

not married to him.' And then something occurred to him, and Adrian looked at her more closely. 'Are you thinking of marrying him?'

'No. Why should I? I don't want kids. I don't need to be married. I told him that in the beginning.'

'Did he believe you?'

'I think so,' she said, looking pensive.

'What if he needs to be married? He may be more respectable than you are,' Adrian said wisely.

'We'll cross that bridge when we come to it. But for now at least, it's not an option,' she said firmly.

'Why not?'

'I'd have to give up too many closets. Besides, his kids would kill me.'

'That's a possibility, from the sound of it. Anyway, if you change your mind, warn me. If you ever tell me you're getting married, I might keel over from the shock. I want to be sitting down when you tell me.'

'Don't worry,' she said confidently, 'I'm not going to. I may have mellowed. But I'm not crazy.'

'Why is it that I don't believe you?' Adrian said as he shook his head in disbelief over the story she had told him, and left her office.

And as promised, John moved in on Sunday. He took Courtenay to Princeton on Saturday, and Hilary flew back to Rhode Island on Friday night. Two hours after he got back from New Jersey he was at Fiona's house, with half a dozen suitcases, and a bunch of suits over his arm. And three banker's boxes full of files and papers. He said he could bring the rest later. This time she had spent hours making more space for him. It still wasn't enough, considering what he'd brought, but it was an improvement. By Sunday night they were a happy couple, officially living together. His daughters were back in school. Mrs. Westerman had the apartment to herself, and Fifi ruled the roost. And in Fiona's house, she and John were comfortable and happy. Sir Winston even wagged his stubby little tail when he saw him. The transition had been surprisingly easy. Another chapter in their life had begun. Everything seemed to be moving very quickly.

Everything continued to go smoothly until Thanksgiving. Inevitably, the issue of the holidays came up, and John and his daughters got in a huge battle over whether or not Fiona would be allowed to join them. Both girls threatened not to come home if she was there. In deference to their family, Fiona insisted on bowing out, and after endless battles with his girls that got him nowhere, John reluctantly agreed to it. She was planning to have Thanksgiving at Adrian's with a large group of his friends, and she told John honestly that she preferred it. She couldn't think of anything more depressing than spending the holiday among people who didn't want her there. And even if John did, his daughters didn't. Not to mention Mrs. Westerman and Fifi. It was a stupid situation, but the best they could do at the moment. And John was deeply grateful for her understanding.

She had a good time with Adrian and their friends. And John had a solemn, lonely Thanksgiving with his two daughters, and the stern-faced housekeeper grimly serving dinner. The meal was anything but happy. And as he and Ann had both been only children, and had lost their parents when they were young, they had no other relatives to share it with them. The holiday only served to make the girls miss their mother more acutely. It was dismal. And at the end of the silent meal, John confronted them and told them that he was tired of their punishing him not only for their mother's death, but also for his relationship with Fiona.

'I'm not going to let you do this,' he said sternly, as both girls cried and told him they didn't want him to forget their mother.

'How can you even say that?' he said, looking offended. 'I loved her. I still do. I always will. I could never forget her or the happy times we shared. But that doesn't mean I have to be alone for the rest of my life, to remember her better. You two are gone now, you're in college. I'm alone here. And I want to be with Fiona. She's a wonderful woman.'

'No, she's not,' Hilary spat at him. 'She's never even been married or had children.'

'That doesn't make her a bad person. Maybe she didn't find the right man.'

'She was too busy working,' Courtenay added, as though they knew her, which they didn't. They had made every effort possible not to.

'That's no reason to punish her. Or me. And that's what you've both been doing. That's not fair to me.'

'Are you going to marry her?' Hilary asked, looking panicked. Fiona had been designated as the enemy, and they were determined to hate her, for no rational reason. They had never given her a chance, and they didn't intend to. But he had no intention of letting them run his life.

'I don't know,' their father said honestly. 'I don't think she wants to get married. She likes her life the way it is. And maybe she's right. After the way you two have behaved, why would she want a family like us, or stepchildren like you? She's better off single.' They both looked faintly embarrassed. Hilary had admitted to one of her roommates the week before how rotten they'd been to her, and she was actually proud of it. Her sister was equally determined.

'We don't want her as a stepmother,' Hilary concluded.

'You could do a lot worse,' John said firmly. 'A lot worse. She's a good woman. And it's not up to you. It's up to me. You're not children. You're nineteen and twenty-one. You don't get to act like this forever. If you want to, it's your business. But I'm not going to let you ruin my life.'

'We won't come home for holidays if you marry

her,' Courtenay said petulantly, sounding like a five-year-old and not a sophomore at Princeton.

'I'm sorry to hear that. You might find yourself in slightly different circumstances,' he said, threatening them subtly, and they both got the message.

'Would you cut us off?' They were checking how far they could go, and as far as he was concerned, they had gone far enough. In fact, way too far.

'I wouldn't test those limits if I were you. I'd be very disappointed in you if you continued to behave this way, if Fiona and I got married.' What he said to them that night sent them scurrying back to the kitchen after dinner, for a consultation with Mrs. Westerman. It sounded like he was going to marry Fiona, from everything he'd said.

'We'd have her out of here in six months if he did,' Mrs. Westerman said confidently as the two girls listened. It sounded like a good plan to them. They liked the idea of getting rid of her in six months. At least they wouldn't be stuck with her forever, and they'd have their father to themselves again. It was all they wanted. If their mother wasn't alive, they didn't want anyone else to take her place. Ever.

'What if he fired you?' Courtenay asked, looking nervous. Other than their father, she was all they had now, and she knew it.

'Let him. I'd go back to North Dakota, and you could come and stay with me whenever you wanted.' She had some money saved, and she had inherited a small house there. He couldn't do anything to her. She had lost respect for him now anyway. She thought what he was doing with that woman just wasn't Christian.

'We don't want you to go away,' Hilary said unhappily. 'We want you to stay forever.' But Mrs. Westerman herself knew that one day she would retire and go home. One of these days the girls would be grown up and married. They were already in college. It wouldn't be long now. And if she kept him from marrying that woman, at least she would have done her duty by the late Mrs. Anderson. She had made her that promise after she died, that she would keep him from defiling her memory, or doing anything foolish. She owed her that much. And she was going to do whatever it took to protect her. Ann Anderson had been such a good woman. And that other woman, the one he was chasing after and sleeping with and making a fool of himself with, well, whoever and whatever he thought she was, as far as Mrs. Westerman was concerned, she was no one. And as long as Rebecca Westerman was alive, Fiona would never get him. It was a solemn vow she had made and would keep no matter what.

10

In spite of the strain between John and his daughters, things were remarkably peaceful between him and Fiona. Their adjustment to living together full time seemed effortless, and she tried to keep the chaos in her life down to a dull roar, so she didn't upset him. She tried to get Jamal to dress more respectably, and not run around the house vacuuming in harem pants and loincloths. And when people dropped by, as they had for years, she suggested that they call her first in future.

She staged no shoots in the house, didn't let it out as a backdrop, as she had before, and no longer allowed photographers from out of town to stay there. She was, if nothing else, trying to be respectful of John. He led a different life than hers, and she couldn't be quite as free and easy as she had been while living by herself. She had taken Adrian's advice, and she wanted John to be happy. The only place where she drew the line was over Sir Winston. She wouldn't have made any changes about the dog. He still slept on her bed, and was as spoiled as any child. But fortunately John had come to love him and found him funny. And she only had a tiny scar on her ankle, courtesy of Fifi. She had never gone to his apartment again. She found it depressing anyway. He only went there when one of his daughters came to town for the weekend, which was seldom. They were busy at school. And they never mentioned Fiona, nor did he. But he still thought it was a miserable situation, and wanted to change it. He just didn't know how to convince them, or win them over. Mrs. Westerman kept the embers hot and the fires burning, whenever she spoke to them. She reminded them that their first loyalty had to be to their mother. It was a vendetta Mrs. Westerman was hell-bent on pursuing. And after her years of kindness and loyalty to them, and the girls' attachment to her, John didn't have the heart to send her back to North Dakota, although he would have liked to. And since the dog had been Ann's, he didn't have the heart to do anything about her either.

He was planning to stay at the apartment with the girls for a week over Christmas. After that, Hilary and Courtenay were going skiing in Vermont with friends, and he and Fiona were going to the Caribbean over New Year's. They were going to St. Bart's, and stopping in Miami on the way home. He had an important new client in Miami, and she wanted to look around South

Beach for the magazine. They were planning to be gone for two weeks. He had already promised to spend Christmas Eve with Fiona, and Christmas Day with his daughters. It was a hell of a way to live, but he had no choice for the moment. It was a tenuous peace between two camps, but nothing was perfect. His life with Fiona was as close as he'd ever gotten to real happiness. He was truly happy with her. And Adrian said he had never seen her look better. Work was going well for both of them, and in spite of the awkwardness of it, they even managed Christmas.

The Christmas Eve he spent with Fiona was peaceful and perfect, and after she went to bed, he went back to the apartment, and was there when his daughters woke up in the morning. He missed Fiona all night, but for the moment, it was a sacrifice he was willing to make for his children. Much to his chagrin, they never thanked him once for it. He and Mrs. Westerman maintained a cool distance. She looked at him now as though he were the incarnation of the devil.

But at least he and the girls enjoyed a nice Christmas Day. They loved the gifts he had gotten for them, and had each gone to a lot of trouble to find something meaningful for him. But their Christmases were always tainted now by the absence of their mother. And late that night, after they had gone out with friends, he slipped out to visit Fiona. Whenever he wasn't with her, he really missed her. She was already asleep in bed with Sir

Winston when he got there. Selfishly, he couldn't resist waking her, and making love to her. And then he left again, to go back to the apartment he stayed at with his daughters. But Fiona's house was home now. He knew he couldn't live this way for much longer. It was a divided life, and the running back and forth seemed so pointless. He had thought about it a lot recently, and he could only think of one solution. What he didn't know was how Fiona would feel about it.

The day after Christmas the girls left for Vermont, and that night he and Fiona flew to St. Martin, and then caught a puddle-jumper to St. Bart's. They stayed in a lovely old French hotel, and it was wonderful being there, with the heat and the sun and the good weather. It was yet another perfect vacation, and it only served to strengthen his resolve, and give him courage. He didn't want to rock the boat, but he also wanted to know that the boat was his now. He no longer wanted to simply charter. And on New Year's Eve, as he toasted her, she saw something odd in his eyes and suddenly got worried.

'Are you okay?' she asked with a look of concern. They had lain on the beach all day, and had made love that night before they went out to dinner.

'Very much so. I have something I want to ask you.' She couldn't imagine what it was, and thought he was teasing her about something. He had a mischievous sense of humor, just as she did.

'You want to know if I love you or Sir Winston more, I'll bet. You know, that just isn't a fair question. He and I have been together longer. But I love you nearly as much. And given time, who knows, I could grow to love you almost as much as I love Sir Winston,' she teased him.

'Will you marry me, Fiona?'

She could see in his eyes that he meant it. Her mouth opened and shut silently, and she stared at him in obvious consternation. 'Oh, shit. You mean that, don't you?'

'Yes, I do. That's not exactly the response I expected.' He looked worried and somber.

'Why did you do that? Why did you ask me?' She looked upset, and so did he now. 'I told you in the beginning, I don't need to be married. Things are fine the way they are. And if I married you, your daughters would put a contract out on me. And your housekeeper would sic the Hound of the Baskervilles on me. I don't need the aggravation. And neither do you,' she said, looking unhappy. This was not the answer he had hoped for.

'This is none of their business. This is about us. Mrs. Westerman is an employee. And my daughters are going to have to accept that I have a right to be happy and have my own life. They have theirs now. Never mind them. What about you? What do you want? Do you want me?' He couldn't have put it more simply, and that touched her.

'Of course I do. But I already have you, don't I? Do we need papers to prove it?'

'Maybe we do. I think I do,' he said honestly. 'I don't like just camping out at your house, feeling like a guest, trying to find an empty closet. Besides, I figure I'll never get a decent closet in that house unless I build one, and it's rude to do that in someone else's house. It's a serious problem.' But as far as Fiona was concerned, so was marriage. Very serious. More serious than she had ever wanted.

'If I let you build a closet, do you still need to get married?' He could see that she looked frightened.

'Why are you so afraid of marriage?' He had never understood it. But she was phobic about it.

'If you get married, people leave each other, and die. They hurt and disappoint each other. They walk out. If all you do is live together, they just get bored with each other at some point, but they don't do as much damage on the way out.' It was all about the father who had abandoned them, he knew, but it was even deeper than that now. She didn't want to be owned, or to risk losing someone she loved. She wanted to hang on lightly. Marriage seemed too tight a grip to her, and she was afraid of being strangled. Even the situation with his daughters would be worse if they got married, and become more important. Now it was his problem, married it would be hers as well. This way she could sympathize with him, and just ignore it. If she married him, she'd have to own it.

'I like being married,' he said honestly. 'I like

what it means. It means I believe in you and will love you forever.'

'There is no forever,' she said softly. His late wife had proven that to him. People had been proving that to her all her life. There was no forever. There was only now. And they already had that. She didn't want to believe in forever, with anyone, it would only hurt her in the end.

'Yes, there is, Fiona. Or close enough. I want to be with you forever.'

'You mean that now,' she said quietly, 'and you think there is. But one day if you get mad at me or fed up, you'll walk out. And if you do, it's simpler this way.'

'Don't you have more faith in me than that?' he asked sadly.

'In you maybe, but not in life. Life doesn't give you forever. It just doesn't.'

'I've never walked out on anyone in my life. And I'm not going to walk out on you. I'm not that kind of person,' he said gently.

'That's what you say now. But who knows what you'd say later. I like it better this way.' She just couldn't do it. And she couldn't see a reason to. Why spoil a good thing with the risk of marriage? It was way too scary. But she didn't want to hurt his feelings either, and she was flattered that he had asked her.

'I don't want to be a guest in your house forever. I want to own something with you, to share a life with you.' He didn't want to say it to her, and he didn't want to frighten her even more, but he would even have liked to have children with her. But he knew how she felt about that. All he wanted now was to be married to her, they could see about the rest later. He didn't want to frighten her even more than she was. There was terror in her eyes. 'Will you think about it?'

'Why?'

'Because I love you. And I want to be married to you.'

'It's such a silly thing to do. Some guy saying words over us isn't going to make us love each other more, or wearing a ring that you give me. I already love you.' He had a ring in his pocket for her, but he didn't want to tell her, or scare her off completely. He had never known another woman like her, but that was why he loved her.

'It's the promise. The commitment. It's a way of saying to the world that I believe in you, and you believe in me, and we're proud of each other.'

'I *am* proud of you. I don't need to be married to you to be proud of you.'

'Maybe I do.' He didn't say more about it after that, and they made love when they went back to their room that night. Afterward, he fell asleep next to her, and she lay in bed thinking about what he had said, trying to imagine what it would be like being married to him. And for once, for some strange reason, it felt comfortable, instead of scary. And then she thought of what Adrian had said to her, about compromise, and maybe if it meant that much to him, and truly made no difference to her, it was something worth doing. She lay in bed and thought about it all night, and she fell asleep finally when the sun came up, and in the morning, she felt strangely peaceful.

He was lying next to her, looking at her when she woke up, and she smiled at him. She had never loved anyone as she loved him, and maybe he was right. She didn't need the paperwork, but maybe it was the right thing to do, to stand beside him and let the world know how much she loved him. But more than anything, she knew it was a way of saying to him the one thing she had never said to anyone, and sworn she never would, it was a way of saying 'I trust you.' That was the core of it for her. She had loved a few men in her life, but she had never trusted anyone, and she did him. Maybe now it was time to prove it.

'You remember that thing you asked me last night,' she said in a whisper as she lay next to him.

'Mmmm . . . yeah . . .' He smiled at her. 'I think I remember.' He was expecting another one of her speeches about why she didn't need marriage. 'What about it?'

'I think I'd like to do it.' She said it so softly, he almost didn't hear it.

'Are you serious?' he whispered back. He had no idea what had made her agree finally. He was stunned.

'Yeah. I think so. Maybe it's not such a bad idea. Just one time. With you. Generally speaking, it's against my principles, but for you, I was thinking of making an exception.'

'That'll do.' He was beaming at her. She only had to be brave about it once. That was generally the best way. One time only. 'Will you really marry me, Fiona?' After everything she'd said to try and talk him out of it, he hardly dared to believe it.

'Yes, I think so. Unless I come to my senses.'

'Maybe we should do it soon, before you do that.'

'When were you thinking?'

'Whenever you want.' He wanted to make it as easy and painless as possible for her.

'Maybe in a few weeks, after we get home. Just the two of us. And maybe Sir Winston.'

'Do I have to marry the dog too?'

'Absolutely.' She looked as though she meant it, and he wasn't about to argue with her. He was much too excited, and much too happy. 'Are you going to tell your children before we do it?' She looked understandably worried.

'I don't think so. They're not going to want to be there. I'd rather tell them after. What do you think?'

'I'd like that better. We can have a party afterward or something. But I think when we actually do "the deed,"' she hated to even say the word, 'it should be private.'

'Name the day, and I'll be there,' he said, and held her close to him, and then he got out of bed, fished the ring out of his pocket, and slipped it on her finger. She lay in bed staring at it in wonder and amazement, and then tears slid slowly down her cheeks as she looked at him. She had finally dared, and finally trusted him enough to do it. Or she was going to, anyway. All she could do then was lie in bed and hold him, knowing how much she loved him. She felt as though she had come home finally, to someone she was truly safe with. She knew that she could trust this man with her heart, and her life, without question.

11

Their wedding day was as simple and as easy as they could possibly have made it. One day after work, they went to get the license. Then Fiona made an appointment with a minister she knew, and on a Saturday afternoon in January, she and John went to a little church she had always liked in the Village. They took a cab downtown, and she brought Sir Winston with her. It was not the kind of wedding John would have planned, but it was exactly what Fiona wanted. She came downstairs wearing a white suit, and a fur coat she seldom wore, and she wore her hair sleek and straight and long. She had never looked as beautiful as when they exchanged their vows in the tiny church, and he put a simple gold ring on her finger. And as she looked up at him, she actually believed, finally, that she belonged to him forever, and he belonged to her. She had never realized how much this would mean to her. To Fiona, it was a promise never to be broken, and she knew that to John it was just as powerful, which was why she had married him. It was a solemn vow they both believed in. And when they went home that afternoon, they just sat there for a while and drank champagne, and then she started to giggle.

'I can't believe I did it,' she said in disbelief.

'Neither can I. I'm so glad you did. *We* did,' he corrected. They decided not to call his children till the next morning. They didn't want to do anything to spoil it.

They spent the night in bed, holding each other, and made love, and everything around them seemed to be quiet and peaceful. And when they woke up in the morning, it was snowing and the entire world was covered in a beautiful white blanket.

They made breakfast and walked the dog, and John looked at her with amusement.

'By the way, what's your name now? Just so I know when I introduce you.'

'What do you think? Does Fiona Anderson sound too weird? Fiona Monaghan-Anderson sounds too pretentious. I'll tell you what, I'll try Anderson for a few weeks, and if I like it, I'll stick with it.'

'That sounds sensible. I have to admit, I hope you like it.'

'We could trade names,' she said, feeling giddy.

After they got back to the house, she called Adrian, and John went upstairs to call his daughters. Both calls were predictable. Adrian was beside himself, he was so thrilled, and both girls were nasty to their father. He knew they had hoped to stop him by their antics, and they were horrified to find they hadn't. But there was nothing they could do to him now. He had married Fiona, and he hoped they would make their peace with it, but even if they didn't, it wouldn't change anything. Fiona didn't ask a lot of questions about it after he had talked to them. She hadn't expected them to react any differently. Adrian had asked her if she was still going to Paris for the January couture shows.

'Of course I am. I didn't quit my job, I just got married,' she said. It had only taken her forty-two years to do it. It was utterly amazing.

But they barely had time to celebrate it. Fiona said that they had taken the honeymoon before the wedding, when they went to the Caribbean. She left for Paris ten days later for the spring/summer couture shows. And right after she got back, they had the ready-to-wear shows during fashion week. Hell week, as she called it. She was working constantly, and scarcely saw John at all for the first month they were married. They didn't even have time to plan a party. And now when his daughters came home, he told them that they could either stay with him at Fiona's, or he and Fiona would both come home, but he was no longer willing to come home alone to see them.

And much to Fiona's horror, the girls reluctantly accepted the idea that she would come with him, and John actually begged her to stay at his apartment for the weekend. She knew how important it was to him. It was one of those hideous sacrifices Adrian had spoken of, which made all the difference, so she agreed to do it. And it was almost as unpleasant as she had expected.

The girls hardly spoke to her, and when they did, they were supercilious and bitchy, but at least they tolerated her being there, which was an improvement. Mrs. Westerman damn near poisoned her with a curry so spicy it nearly killed her, and much to John's horror and disbelief, she 'accidentally' let Fifi out of the kitchen, and the dog made a beeline straight to Fiona's left leg this time, and took a chunk out of her left ankle, instead of the right one. This time she only needed four stitches. Adrian looked at her in total astonishment when he saw her on Monday morning.

'Again? Are you insane? When are they going to put that dog down?'

'I thought John was going to kill the house-keeper. He screamed so loud that both girls were crying, and she threatened to quit. I may have to get a stun gun the next time the girls come to visit.'

'I hope they don't come often. Did he fire the housekeeper?'

'He can't. The girls love her.'

'Fiona, she's trying to kill you.'

'I know. Death by fatal curry. I still have heart-burn from it. Thank God the dog is too short to go for my throat, otherwise she would. I just have to make the best of it. I love him.'

'You don't have to love the dog, his house-keeper, and his children.'

'That's a much bigger challenge,' she confessed, and John was once again mortally embarrassed. It had been a pretty ghastly weekend, and he had been having a lot of stress at the office. Fiona had been busier than she'd been in months. The whole magazine seemed to be going crazy. People had quit, the format had changed, the new ad campaign was causing problems and had to be redesigned, which was yet another of John's problems, as well as hers. A photographer had sued the magazine. A supermodel had OD'd on a shoot and damn near died, and attracted a huge amount of negative publicity. Fiona was coming home at ten o'clock every night, and traveling more than she ever had. She made three trips to Paris in one month, and the following month she got stuck in Berlin for two weeks, and then had to fly right back out to Rome for an important meeting with Valentino. John complained that he never saw her, and he was right.

'I know, sweetheart, I'm so sorry. I don't know what's happened. I can't seem to get things calmed down. Every time I solve one problem, I get hit with another.' But his office was no calmer than hers was. The agency was changing hands again, and it was causing him huge problems. And in April, one of his daughters told him she was pregnant, and had an abortion. She blamed him, and said that if he hadn't married Fiona, she wouldn't have been so freaked out, and wouldn't have been careless with the boy she slept with. It was ridiculous to blame him, but John somehow felt guilty and blamed himself, and indirectly, when he had too much to drink one night, he blamed Fiona, which shocked her.

'Do you really believe that? That Hilary's abortion is my fault, and the pregnancy?' Fiona stared at him in disbelief.

'I don't know what to believe. We upset the hell out of them. And dammit, Fiona, I never see you.' He was most unhappy about that.

'What does that have to do with anything?'

'I feel like I'm living with a flight attendant. You come here to change clothes and pack another suitcase. And take off again. And I'm stuck here with your fucking dog and that half-naked lunatic who runs around in a gold lamé Speedo when I come home from the office. I need a little more sanity around here than I'm getting. I need to come home to a normal house, with all the stresses I have at the office.'

'Then you should have married a normal person,' she snapped back at him. The things he had said to her had been hurtful.

'I thought I did. I can't live with all this chaos.'

'What chaos?' She hardly entertained anymore. Her salons had dwindled down to nothing, because she didn't want to upset him. And she promised to tell Jamal to keep his clothes on. She had told him that before, but whenever she wasn't around, he did what he wanted. But there was no harm in it, and he was a sweet man.

Adrian noticed how furious she looked when she came to work one morning, and she told him about it. She and John had just had yet another argument about Jamal.

'I told you you'd need to compromise. Buy Jamal a uniform, and tell him he has to wear it.'

'What difference does it make? Who cares what he wears when he vacuums?'

'John does,' Adrian said sternly. 'And what did you do about the closets?'

'I haven't had time to do anything. I've been on airplanes for three months. I haven't had a break, Adrian, and you know it.'

'Well, you'd better do something. You don't want to lose him.'

'I'm not going to lose him,' she said confidently. 'We're married.'

'Since when did that give anyone a guarantee?'

'Well, it's supposed to,' she said, looking stubborn. 'That's what the vows are supposed to mean, isn't it?'

'Sure, if you marry a saint. With humans, the warranty may run out. Fiona, people get impatient.' He tried to warn her.

'Okay, okay, I'll give him a closet. What does he need a closet for anyway? He left most of his clothes at the apartment. Along with his wife's, and that portrait of her I hate. We had an argument about it the other day. He wants to bring it to my house, so the girls feel at home there. For chrissake, why in God's name would I want to live with his wife's portrait?'

'Compromise, compromise, compromise!' Adrian wagged a finger at her. 'He has a point. It might make his kids like you better. You can put it in their bedroom. You don't have to see it.'

'I'm not turning my house into a shrine to his late wife. I can't live like that either.'

'The first year is always the hardest,' Adrian said calmly, but that was because he wasn't the one compromising. But neither was Fiona. She wanted to keep everything as it had been, and every time John moved something, or changed something, she had a fit when she came home from the office. And she told Jamal not to let John change anything. So they had a huge fight when she was in L.A., supervising a shoot of Madonna. John had been putting some of his books in the library, and Jamal wouldn't let him. John had called her in L.A. and threatened to move out if she didn't call Jamal off. It was the first time he had done that, and she was frightened and told Jamal to let him do whatever he wanted. Jamal had argued with her on the phone, that she had told him not to let John change anything, and she nearly got hysterical screaming at him, and told him to just do what she told him and not make more problems. Jamal called her in tears that night and threatened to quit, and she begged him not to. She wanted familiar people, places, and things

177

around her. And suddenly everything was changing. She had two stepdaughters she couldn't stand, and a man who wanted to make his mark in her life, and had a right to. But after a lifetime of doing things her way, and controlling her environment, she felt every change he wanted to make like an assault on her person. Even seeing his books in her library unnerved her slightly. He had put some of hers on a top shelf, to make room for his own.

It was as though they were constantly at each other's throats these days, arguing and shouting and accusing. Mrs. Westerman had threatened to quit, John was thinking of selling the apartment, and his daughters were outraged. And if he did sell it, Fiona knew his daughters would come to stay at her place. And whatever happened, she was not willing to take the dog. She had threatened to put it down if he brought it to her house, and he had said something about it to Hilary and Courtenay, and now they hated her more. It was an endless vicious circle of misunderstandings and misquotes, and raw nerves, and constantly stressful situations, for all concerned.

In April, things took a dramatic turn for the worse, when John told her he was organizing a dinner party for a new client. He wanted to do it at Le Cirque, in a private room, and asked Fiona to help. His secretary wasn't good at that sort of thing, and it seemed reasonable to him to ask Fiona to give him a hand. All he wanted her to do was book the room, choose the menu, order the flowers, and help him with the seating. He had to invite several people from the agency, and at least one member of the creative staff, and it was a somewhat awkward group. He knew the client fairly well, but had never met his wife, and he trusted Fiona's judgment about the details, and how to seat the party. The client was an extremely dour man from the Midwest, and about as far from Fiona's world as you could get.

The first thing Fiona did was insist they have it at her house. She said it would have a more personal touch, and be considerably less stuffy. She insisted it would put everyone at ease, rather than doing it at a restaurant, which seemed more impersonal to her, although they both loved Le Cirque.

'I always do business dinners here for the magazine,' she insisted, and John said he was uneasy about it.

'The people you entertain for the magazine are a lot different. You've never seen anyone more uptight than this guy. And I know nothing about his wife.'

'Trust me. I know what I'm doing,' she said confidently, determined to redeem herself for the stress of the past months. 'I'll treat them like visiting dignitaries. I'll get my caterer to do it. If you want, we can do fabulous French food like Le Cirque.'

'What about Jamal?' he asked nervously. 'This guy was the head of the Republican Party in

Michigan before he moved here. I don't think he'd understand a house man in harem pants, and I don't want him to think we're weird.'

'He has a uniform. I'll make him wear it. I promise. I'll threaten his life,' she reassured him, and meant it. She had bought him a proper butler's uniform after she'd married John, anticipating an evening such as this, and she had wanted to be prepared. He'd never worn it yet, but she knew it fit him. She had made him try it on, and had had it tailored for him. She called the caterers the next day, the florist, ordered fancy French food for the menu, and exquisite wines. She was going to serve Haut-Brion, Cristal, Cheval Blanc, and Château d'Yquem for dessert. She was determined to make up for all past sins that night, and was absolutely certain everything would go fine. She was leaving nothing to chance.

The day of the dinner party, she had a major crisis at the magazine, and two of her best editors threatened to quit over a layout that hadn't gone well and Fiona had been forced to pull. She had World War III in the office, her secretary announced that she was pregnant, and threw up all day. And Adrian was out with the flu. She had a massive headache herself by mid-afternoon, which was threatening to become a migraine. As soon as she got home, she took a pill she found in her medicine cabinet in an unmarked bottle that someone had given her in Europe. It was relatively mild and had worked before. Everything was in control. And half an hour before the dinner party, the caterers had everything in order, Jamal was wearing his uniform, the table looked beautiful, and the crystal and glass shone. And when John checked it all out before the guests arrived, he looked relieved and pleased. The table looked like a layout in a magazine. It was perfect, and the food smelled delicious.

The guest of honor and his wife arrived right on time, in fact they were five minutes early, which Fiona found slightly unnerving. She was just zipping up a plain black dress when the doorbell rang, and John hurried downstairs. She put on high-heeled black satin pumps, and a pair of big coral earrings. She looked so simple and respectable, she barely recognized herself, as she glanced in the mirror and went down to join their guests. She still had the headache, but was feeling better since she'd taken the pill, and she smiled warmly at John's client, when John introduced her first to Matthew Madison, and then to his extremely uptight wife. Neither of them looked as though they had cracked a smile in years. The rest of the guests took a little of the stiffness out of it as they arrived one by one. There were to be ten guests in all, and with Fiona and John, it made twelve.

Jamal passed the first plate of hors d'oeuvres, and everything went fine, just as Fiona felt her headache returning with a vengeance. John's obvious concern over the evening didn't help, and she felt stressed just watching him. He wanted everything to be perfect, and it was. Fiona decided not to take another pill for her headache. She quietly asked Jamal for a glass of champagne instead. And by the time she finished the glass, it seemed to help. She went to put some music on to add some atmosphere, and smiled to herself. She hadn't given a dinner party as proper and restrained as this in years. Or ever. She liked things livelier and more fun, and definitely more exotic. But she wanted to do everything just the way John had asked her to, and she had.

It was when Jamal passed the hors d'oeuvres the second time that she saw John signal her and point to him, and she couldn't understand what he was saying. He was frowning at her ferociously, and then glancing at Jamal's feet. And then she saw that along with his black trousers with the satin stripe down the side, and the proper black tux jacket, white shirt, and bow tie he had worn, he had added a pair of gold and rhinestone high heels after the party began. She recognized them immediately, they were hers. She followed him into the kitchen and told him he had to take them off.

'Why aren't you wearing proper shoes?' she chided him as they stood whispering in the kitchen, and he looked at her innocently and shrugged.

'They hurt.'

'So do those. I get blisters every time I wear

them. Jamal, you have to take them off. John is having a fit.'

'I hate men's shoes, they're so ugly,' he said, looking unhappy.

'I don't care. Tonight is important. Change your shoes.'

'I can't.'

'Why not?'

'I threw them away.'

'Where?'

'In the garbage.' She pulled the top off the garbage can, and there they were, with oyster shells, two empty cans of caviar, and half a tomato aspic that had gone wrong lying on them. There was no way he could wear the shoes. She was about to suggest John's, but his feet were nearly four sizes larger than Jamal's.

'Go upstairs and get a pair of my flats at least. Black ones!' she urged, as he ran up the back stairs, still wearing her gold high heels. She had another quick glass of champagne then, and went back out to John and his extremely boring guests. And as she walked into the living room, she tripped, and the contents of her third glass of champagne flew across the room and landed on Sally Madison's dress, as Fiona gasped.

'Oh my God, I'm so sorry, Sammy . . . I mean Sarry . . . Sally . . .' John noticed instantly that she was slurring, and he had never seen her drunk before, so he couldn't imagine what was wrong, as Fiona hurried back to the kitchen to get a towel and some soda water to get the champagne off the woman's dress.

The evening went downhill swiftly after that. Jamal returned wearing different shoes, as he'd been told, but instead of black, he had chosen shocking pink alligator flats. It wasn't what Fiona had had in mind, and everyone in the room noticed it as he passed the hors d'oeuvres. And by the time they sat down to dinner, Fiona was so drunk she could hardly stand up. The seemingly harmless headache pill and the champagne had turned out to be a lethal mix. She had to go upstairs and lie down before dessert. The food was good and the wine was excellent, but Jamal had clearly shocked the Madisons and continued to do so as he served the meal, and chatted amiably with the guests. And John wanted to assure them he was going to send his wife to Betty Ford. John was ready to kill her by the time the guests left.

He was absolutely furious when he went upstairs and found her sprawled on their bed still in her dress, and she woke almost as soon as he walked in.

'Oh my God, I have the most god-awful headache,' she said with a groan as she rolled over, looked up at him, and put both her hands on her head.

'Why the hell did you do that?' he asked her in a fury. She had never seen him as angry, and hoped she never would again. 'How could you get drunk at a dinner as important as that? For chrissake, Fiona, you acted like a candidate for AA.'

'I had a headache, I took some stupid pill before dinner. I think the champagne made it kick in. It never did that before.' But she'd never added champagne to it before either.

'What was it?' He glared at her angrily. 'Heroin? And what was Jamal doing? Smoking crack when he got dressed? What the hell was he doing in those shoes?'

'The gold ones or the pink ones?' She was trying to focus on what John was saying, but she was still very drunk from the pill and the champagne, and five minutes later, in spite of her best efforts to pay attention to what he was saying, she went back to sleep.

She had a massive hangover the next day, and she couldn't remember anything about the dinner, but over breakfast, in icy tones, John filled her in. He didn't speak to her after that for a week. He got the account anyway, much to his amazement, but he called Madison the next day and apologized for his wife's behavior, and hoped she hadn't done any permanent damage to Sally's dress with the spilled champagne. Matthew Madison was surprisingly understanding about it, and John explained that Fiona had made the unfortunate mistake of taking a headache pill and drinking champagne. It was the kind of excuse anyone would make, he realized, for an alcoholic wife. And there was no question, as April drifted into May, that the evening had taken a toll on them. John was still upset about it, although Fiona had apologized a thousand times. Of all times for Fiona to have combined alcohol and medication, that was not the night for it, as far as John was concerned.

And in May, during an important shoot that lasted a week, a world-famous photographer got thrown out of his hotel for arguing with the manager, and bringing five call girls to his room at one time, which had upset the other guests. Fiona had no choice, she felt, but to bring him to her house, and settle him in her guest room, which meant that all the rolling racks of her clothes found their way into the living room. There was utter chaos in the house when John came home from the office, and found the photographer, two hookers, and a drug dealer who sold him cocaine, in the living room, having sex. Fiona was still at work. John went absolutely berserk, justifiably, and threw them all out. He was shaking with rage when he called Fiona in the office. She didn't blame him, and she was upset too, but the photographer was one of the most important she dealt with, and she didn't want him to quit, which he did the next day, and flew back to Paris. She had no idea how to fill the gap in the July issue. She was sitting in her office in tears over it when Adrian walked in, and she shouted at him.

'If you tell me to compromise one more time, I'm going to kill you. That idiot Pierre St. Martin had an orgy in my living room last night, and John

186

threw him out. He just quit and destroyed the whole goddamn July issue. And three weeks ago, I got drunk on champagne and a French headache pill at a business dinner I gave for John at the house. We're driving each other insane. His wife's portrait is in my living room, his children hate me, and it's my fault his daughter had an abortion. And what the hell am I going to do with the July issue? That sonofabitch quit and left me holding the bag when John threw his ass out in the street, and I don't blame him. He was screwing his drug dealer and two hookers when John came home from the office. I would have gone nuts too. And he still hasn't forgiven me for getting drunk at his dinner. I had a migraine. And Jamal wore my gold Blahnik shoes with the six-inch heels from last season.' It was a litany of woes.

'Oh my God. Fiona, he's going to kill you if he has to put up with shit like that. Your life is out of control.'

'I know. I love him, but I can't deal with his children, and he wants me to love them. They're nasty rotten spoiled brats, and I hate them.'

'But they're *his* nasty rotten spoiled brats, and he does love them,' Adrian interrupted. 'And now they're yours too, and love them or not, you have to put up with them because you love him. And don't take any more photographers into the house, for God's sake.'

'Now you tell me,' she said miserably as she blew her nose.

'Maybe you should get rid of Jamal too, and hire a normal maid.'

'I can't. He's been with me forever. That wouldn't be fair.'

'It's not fair to expect John to live with your half-naked house man running all over the house in gold lamé shorts and your shoes. It's embarrassing for him. What if he brings someone home from the office?' She worried about it, which was why she'd bought him the uniform, but she knew Jamal needed her, and he was so loyal and kindhearted. It seemed so mean to fire him. She couldn't see why John couldn't accept him too. 'You're not making this easy for John, Fiona,' Adrian chided her as she sat back in her chair and sighed.

'He's not making it easy for me either. He knew what my life was like before he married me. He lived with me, for chrissake.'

'Yes, but it's different once you're married. It's his house now too.'

'He still has his apartment. Why doesn't he take people there if he doesn't want them to see Jamal?' Although she had suggested he give the business dinner at her house, which had seemed like a good idea. It would have been if she hadn't gotten a migraine, taken the pill, and gotten drunk as a result.

'Why should he go to his place? I thought you told me he wanted to sell the apartment.'

'He does, and he wants the girls to stay with us,

which means I'll lose my guest room, and I'll have those monsters right in my house with their killer dog.'

'For God's sake, Fiona, it's only a Chihuahua or something. What is it?' He looked distracted. This was upsetting him too.

'It's a Pekingese. And why are you always on his side?'

'I'm not,' Adrian said calmly. 'I'm on yours, because I know you love him. And if you don't do something about all this, you'll lose him. I don't want that to happen to you.'

'This was exactly what I was afraid of, and why I never got married. I don't want to have to give up me, in order to be his.'

'You don't. Jamal isn't you. You have to give up some of the trimmings. You don't have to give up you.'

'And what does he give up?'

'At this rate, his sanity, to live with you. Look at it from his side. He wants to make his kids feel comfortable with you. He doesn't want to lose his kids for you. You have some goofy house man running around half naked, no matter how sweet he is, which embarrasses John. You have a smelly old dog snoring on his bed every night. You have a job that keeps you running around the world constantly. You have weird friends like me. And you bring in some French lunatic who brings hookers and a drug dealer into his house, and screws them in plain sight in the living room. How sane would you be if someone dragged you into all that and expected you to live with it? Frankly, I love you, but I'd go insane if I lived with you.'

'Okay, okay, I'll clean it up. But the portrait in the living room is a bit much, don't you think?'

'Not if it makes his kids feel at home. Win them over first, you can always move the portrait to their room later.'

'I don't want them to have a room.'

'You married a man with kids. They have to have a room. You have to give in somewhere,' Adrian said relentlessly. He wanted this to work for her, and he was getting worried. So was she.

'This is hard for me,' she said as she blew her nose again. It was suddenly all so stressful, for both of them.

'It's just as hard for him. Give him something. You'll lose him if you don't.' They both knew she didn't want that, but she didn't want to change anything either. She wanted him to get used to all of it. And she wanted his kids to disappear, and they weren't going to do that. If she wanted him, she had to welcome them into her home, no matter how rude they were to her. 'No more photographers in the house,' Adrian warned her. 'Promise me that at least. And buy Jamal a decent pair of men's shoes.' She didn't bother telling Adrian she had and he'd thrown them away because he thought they were ugly.

'Okay, I promise.' That was the easy part. The rest was a lot harder, and she was still mulling it over when she went home that night, and found a note from John. He had gone to his apartment for a few days to get some peace. She called him there, and Mrs. Westerman answered. She said he was out, and Fiona didn't believe her. She called his cell phone, and it was on voice mail. She felt as if he had shut her out, and she felt panicked. Maybe Adrian was right and she had to make some changes quickly.

But she felt as though the fates were conspiring against her. They had an emergency on a shoot in London two days later, and they insisted she had to come over. It was a story on the royal family. She had no choice. She had to go. And this time she was gone for two weeks. She only got to speak to John twice while she was away. He always seemed to be too busy to talk to her, and his cell phone was always on voice mail. When she came back, he was still in his apartment. He said he didn't want to stay at her place while she was away. His girls had been on a break from school, and they'd been at home with him. And in another two weeks, they would both be on vacation for the summer. He startled Fiona by saying that he was going on vacation alone with them. They were going back to the ranch in Montana where he had always taken them with Ann. They were going when she would be in Paris for the haute couture.

'I thought you'd come with me,' she said, looking disappointed and feeling frightened.

'I need to spend some time with them,' he said

191

quietly. And then he ripped her heart out with what he said next. 'Fiona, this isn't working. Our lives are too different. You live with constant chaos and insanity and turmoil. Photographers doing drugs and screwing hookers in your house is just the tip of the iceberg,' he said sternly. But it had also been the last straw for him, especially after the business dinner with her drunk, and Jamal in her gold shoes, followed by the pink ones. It all seemed unimportant and frivolous, but it was too much for him.

'That's not fair. That only happened once,' she said plaintively.

'That's once too often. I can't have people like that around my kids. What if the girls had been there when that fool was having an orgy in our living room? What if they'd walked in?'

'If the girls were around, I wouldn't have let him stay there. He's one of the most important photographers I work with, and I didn't want to lose the shoot.' But she had anyway. And now she was losing him.

'And Jamal is a nice boy. But I don't want him around the girls either. There are a lot of strange characters in your life, and you like that. It's part of your world. But I can't live with all that craziness in my home. I never know who's going to be there when I walk in. The only one who never is anymore is you. You've been gone almost constantly since we got married.' He was beginning to feel she was doing it on purpose to avoid him.

192

'I've had a lot of problems at the magazine,' she said unhappily.

'So have I at the agency. But I don't take it out on you.'

'Yes, you do. This has been a hard time for both of us.'

'Harder than you know,' he said sadly. 'I don't even have a place to hang my suits.'

'I'll give you more closets. We can buy a bigger house if you want. Mine is too small for two people.' And certainly for four, if the girls were moving in too. God forbid.

'There isn't room in your life for two people. Or maybe it's just too weird.'

'If you wanted someone so proper and uptight, why did you marry me?' she said, as tears rolled down her cheeks.

'Because I love you. I did then. And I still do. But I can't live with you. And it's not fair to expect you to change it. This is how you want to live. I was wrong to push you into marriage. I see that now. You've been right to stay free for all these years. You knew what you were doing. I didn't. I guess I wanted to be a part of it. It was exciting. But I realize now it's too exciting for me.'

'What are you saying?' She was horrified and heartbroken. She couldn't believe what she was hearing. He had told her it was forever. And she had trusted him.

'I'm saying that I want a divorce. I'm getting a divorce. I already talked to my lawyer. And I've talked about it with the girls for the last two weeks.'

'You talked about it with them before you talked about it with me?' She looked like a child who had been abandoned on the street, which was what he was about to do to her. Except that she wasn't a child, she was a woman. And he had a right to leave.

'I'll fire Jamal. You can have all my closets. I'll throw away my clothes. Your kids can move in. And I'll never let another photographer stay here again.' She was pleading with him. She didn't want to lose him. The thought of losing him made her feel desperate and sick.

'It would never work. And the bottom line is that I don't want to lose my kids. I will if I stay with you.' Even if they'd been horrible to her, they were still his children, and he loved them. More than he loved her. And under Mrs. Westerman's ever evil influence they had been pressuring him, and blackmailing him emotionally to leave her. And with everything so difficult between him and Fiona it provided fertile ground for the forces against them to dig their heels in. It had worked. They had finally won him over. Fiona had to go.

'They don't have a right to do this. And neither do you.' She was sobbing. She couldn't believe what had happened. Even in her anguish, she knew that some of it was her fault. Maybe even a lot of it. But some of it was his. And he had made a deal with his kids. In the end, they had won. She was going to lose the one man she had really loved. Adrian was right. She hadn't compromised enough. She had felt so safe that she had ignored all the warnings. And now he was going to divorce her, in order to please his kids. But she had made more than her share of mistakes too.

He never came back to her house. The first set of papers arrived two weeks later. The whole affair had lasted eleven months from beginning to end. Almost a year. Not quite. Just long enough to really love him, and have it cost her soul when he left. They had been married for nearly six months. They would be divorced by Christmas. It was all unthinkable. He had promised. He had loved her. They were married. It meant nothing. Marriage was the one thing she had never wanted. And now it was all she wanted. It was all a cruel trick.

Two weeks after she got the papers notifying her that he had filed the papers, she left for Paris for the haute couture.

As he always did, Adrian came with her. He kept her company this time, instead of John. He dragged her from place to place. She was like a ghost. She was so out of it, you could almost see right through her. And Adrian was desperately worried about her. It was as though Fiona, the woman he had known and loved and laughed with and worked with, had entirely disappeared.

12

Fiona did not go to the Hamptons all summer. She stayed at home, nursed her wounds, sat home alone at night, went to the office, and cried often. It was as though all the life had gone out of her, all the joy and excitement and passion. She felt as though she were in a dark tunnel, lost in the darkness. Everything she had hoped for and loved and trusted had been taken from her. And every time she saw Jamal cavorting through the house, she berated herself again for the mistakes she'd made. Right or wrong, she entirely blamed herself. John had shown her all she had ever wanted, and never let herself hope for, and when she failed to understand, he took it all away again. Nothing in her life had ever hurt so much, not even when her mother died, or she lost men later on. The loss of the marriage she had shared with John was the death of hope for her. She was like a naughty child who had been punished. For her poor judgment and foolish ways, she had been given an adult sentence, and put to death, or so she felt. She didn't deserve either the punishment he meted out to her, nor the abuse she heaped on herself afterward, and nothing anyone could do or say made it right for her again. As she dragged through the summer toward September, she could barely work. And on the Labor Day weekend, in crushing heat, disaster struck again. Sir Winston had a heart attack and was on life support for two weeks.

She visited him twice daily, before and after work, stroked his face, kissed his paws, and just sat quietly beside him. And finally, with a snore and a peaceful look at her, he closed his eyes one afternoon and went quietly to sleep for good. It was a peaceful death. And yet one more blow to her. He had been a beloved faithful friend.

Two days later, they had a major meeting with their ad agency, and there was no way she could avoid it. She discussed it with Adrian beforehand, and he said she absolutely had to go, no matter how hard it was for her. She hadn't heard a word from John all summer. When he ended it, he did so for good. The clock was running, and the divorce would be final in three months. After such a short marriage, it shouldn't have been the death blow it was to her, but even Adrian knew now that it was.

She had opened places in herself to him that had never seen light and air and love before, and had never known human touch. And when he shut the door on them, and on her, he created wounds that she had been trying to shield herself from all her life. Worse yet, he had reopened every wound

197

she'd ever had, while creating more. It was a blow of total devastation, and there was no way she could sit through a meeting with him. On the morning it was scheduled to happen, she picked up the phone to call in sick, and then thought better of it. Adrian was right. If only out of self-respect and dignity, she had to go. And what was worse, she wanted to see him, and did.

John Anderson strode into the meeting, looking tanned and handsome and athletic. He was wearing a dark blue pinstriped suit, a crisp white shirt that fit him to perfection, one of his classic navy blue Hermès ties with tiny red dots, and a white handkerchief in his pocket. He looked like a million dollars. And Fiona felt like two cents.

To all who saw her in the meeting, she looked competent, quiet, as elegant as ever. She was every inch in command and control, and she was pleasant and polite when she addressed him. But no one had any idea what it cost her just to be there, or to chat with him for a few minutes on the way out.

'You're looking well, Fiona,' he said politely. But when she looked at him, she saw that there was a self-protective wall all around him, and a shield of ice just behind his eyes. He was not letting her in again, and no one who saw them could have guessed that they'd been married, or that either or both of them were still in love. They both maintained an entirely professional demeanor, although he did notice how thin she'd gotten, and how pale she was. She was wearing a narrow black linen Yohji Yamamoto dress that accentuated her extreme slimness, and her face was the color of snow when they spoke. 'Did you get away at all this summer?' She didn't look it, and if she had, she must have been hiding under a rock. Her skin looked almost translucent it was so white.

'I've been working on this ad campaign,' she said, looking distracted, 'and we always close the December book in August. I've been pretty much working all month,' and in fact, since he left, she felt as dry as a bone, creatively, and hadn't come up with a decent idea in months. She felt washed up, and was. 'How are the girls?'

'Terrific. Hilary is a senior, and Courtenay is doing her junior year abroad. She's in Florence, so I'll be going over to see her whenever I can.' They spoke like two old acquaintances who hadn't met in a long time, instead of two people who had been married and in love. He had completely shut her out. And a moment later, they both moved on.

Adrian had been watching, and spoke to her in a quiet voice as they left the room side by side. 'How was it?' he asked, looking worried.

'How was what?' she asked, pretending not to know what he was talking about.

'I saw you talking to John.'

'It was fine,' she said, turning away to speak to someone else, and then she went back to her office, and successfully avoided him for the rest of the afternoon. Every time Adrian came to her office to discuss something, she pretended to be busy or on the phone. She couldn't speak to anyone, not even him. She was distraught.

It took another month after that for her to make up her mind, after several small disasters in the office, which were a warning signal to her that she could no longer handle not only her life but her job. On all fronts, and in all venues of her life, she was barely hanging on. She didn't even have Sir Winston to go home to at night. She had no one, and nothing, and the funny, crazy, zany free-spirited life she had once loved no longer held any appeal to her. She hated going to work every day, and even more than that she hated coming home.

She handed in her resignation to *Chic* magazine on the first of October, and she knew it was time. She gave them a month's notice, which wasn't long, and in a private letter to the head of the board, she strongly recommended Adrian for her job. She said that she was resigning due to health and personal reasons, and had made a decision to take a year or two off, and move abroad, which wasn't entirely a lie. She was so deeply depressed that she could no longer function, and she had decided to rent her house, and move to Paris for a few months. When she felt better, she wanted to try and write a book.

Adrian stormed into her office the moment it was announced. 'You didn't tell me!' he said, looking hurt and heartbroken. 'Fiona, what have you done?'

'I had to do it,' she said quietly. 'I can't do my job anymore. I think I've lost it. It just doesn't mean anything. I don't give a damn about the people, the parties, the look, or the clothes. I don't care if I never go to a single couture show again, in fact I hope I don't.'

'You could have at least told me before you did it. We could have talked about it. Why didn't you take six months off?' But they both knew that she couldn't do that in her job. She couldn't leave the magazine without a rudder, in fact when she went away for a week, all hell broke loose, and everything got out of control. Two days later he learned that she had recommended him for her job. It was the right decision, and a wise recommendation, and within two weeks of her resignation, Adrian was named editor-in-chief of *Chic* magazine, and they told her that within another week, when the dust had settled, she was free to go. Everything had moved very fast.

She left her office quietly, without a glance over her shoulder. There were tears in her eyes when she walked out, carrying a box of books and a single plant her mentor had given her years before. Adrian was crying openly as he took the box from her. They both knew that the waters closed rapidly over old editors, and they were soon forgotten, but there was no denying that Fiona Monaghan had made her mark, and she had trained him well.

They had wanted to give her a party when she left, but she had declined it. She just wasn't in the mood. Five minutes after she left her office, Adrian put her in a cab and handed her the box he'd been carrying for her.

'I love you,' she whispered as she smiled sadly, and their eyes met and held.

'You're the best friend I ever had.' There were tears in his eyes.

'You too. See you tomorrow.' He was coming to the house in the morning to help her pack. She had already rented her house, and was sending all her furniture to storage. She was taking almost nothing to Paris. She had rented a small room at the Ritz, at a discount they'd offered her, till she found an apartment. Thanks to wise investments over the years, she was in good shape, and wouldn't have to work for a long time. She was going to find an apartment and, if she felt up to it, write a book. Maybe in the spring. Before that she was going to take long walks, sleep a lot, and try to heal. The good news was that she would never have to see John Anderson again. She was going to miss the magazine, she knew, but not nearly as much as she missed him. And she had to forget them both. They were part of the past. The future was unknown and didn't look hopeful to her. And the present was intolerably painful.

Adrian came, as promised, the next morning. It took them all day to empty her closets into wardrobe boxes. She was amazed at what she found there, and at the mountain of once-meaningful out-of-date treasures she gave away.

'You could start a fashion museum with all this stuff,' Adrian said as he dumped another armload on the pile she was giving to Goodwill.

'If I'd done this while John was here, he could have had more than half the closets,' she said ruefully. There was almost nothing left in the closets that had once been crammed full.

'Forget about it,' Adrian said wisely. 'It wasn't about closets. It was about a lot of things. Your lifestyles were too different. He'd been married all his life, you never had been. He had kids, you didn't. His kids hated you, his housekeeper hated you, his dog tried to kill you. Twice. And the people you hung out with drove him insane.' They both knew, as had John eventually, that although he loved her and found her fabulous and exciting, she had been like a hot chili pepper stuck in his windpipe, and a mouthful of wasabi that made his eyes water in terror most of the time. Adrian firmly believed that John had loved her. He had just bitten off more than he could chew. He needed someone a lot more bland than Fiona Monaghan would ever be. But it nonetheless broke Adrian's heart that John had left her so suddenly. It seemed terribly unfair to him. She didn't deserve that, no matter how chaotic her life was.

'Did you tell him about Sir Winston?' Adrian asked, curious, as he dropped fifty pairs of old

Manolos into one of the boxes for Goodwill. The heels were too high even for Jamal. The flat ones she was giving to him. She didn't want to encourage him to wear high heels.

'I didn't think it was any of his business,' she said in answer to Adrian's question about the dog. 'I didn't want to sound pathetic. "Thanks for divorcing me, oh and by the way, my dog died too."' She had paid five thousand dollars to bury him in a pet cemetery, and for a heart-shaped black granite tombstone, which she had never seen. She couldn't bear to go out and visit him.

Adrian came back to help her again on Sunday. And she spent the rest of the following week disposing of her things. In honor of her own sense of the ridiculous, she left for Paris on Halloween.

Adrian took her to the airport, and they stood looking at each other for a long moment before she went through security.

'Be good to yourself. Stop beating yourself up. Things happen for a reason.' Yeah. Her father leaving. Her mother dying. John divorcing her. Sir Winston dying. Giving up a job that had once meant everything to her. Now none of it meant anything. 'And call me. I worry about you.'

'Do a good job,' she said with tears in her eyes as she left him. She knew he would. He was every bit as good an editor as she, and he had a lot more life in him than she did at this point. 'Make me proud of you.' She was anyway.

'I love you,' he said, with tears rolling down his

204

cheeks. Their faces were awash with tears as they kissed, both his and hers. 'Knock 'em dead in Paris. I'll see you in January, or before if I can get away.' January seemed like an eternity to both of them. The haute couture shows were nearly three months away. And the big problem for her was that she had been knocked dead in New York, far too effectively. She felt as though they should be putting her on the flight in a body bag, not a seat. She had never felt as awful in her life.

'Take care,' she whispered, as she put her head down and walked away, blinded by tears. He stood there for as long as he could see her, with tears rolling down his cheeks.

13

The room Fiona had rented at the Ritz was small and almost womblike for her, and had a view of the winter sky. She sat staring up at it sometimes, missing everyone and everything, John, Adrian, her job, her house, New York, Sir Winston, even Jamal. In a matter of months, she had lost everything, and now she was here, not sure what to do next. The winter in Paris was rainy and gray, but it suited her mood, and she was glad she was there. She didn't need to talk to anyone, or see anyone. In fact, she didn't want to. She was steeped in her own solitude and grief.

In mid-December, the divorce papers reached her in Paris. It didn't matter anymore. Nothing did. She spent Christmas Eve and Christmas Day in her room. She went to mass at Sacré Coeur and a choir of nuns sang so exquisitely, she felt as though she had died and gone to heaven. She sat listening to them, with tears running down her cheeks.

And that night, when she went back to the

hotel, she started to write. It wasn't the book she had thought she would do. It was a book about a little girl, with a childhood like hers, and it followed her into womanhood, the mistakes she made, and the healing she pursued. It was a catharsis of sorts writing it, and things came clearer to her as she did. It was so much easier to see it now, the paths she had chosen, the men she had feared, those she had chosen instead, her determination, her career. The things she had used as substitutes for real relationships, the job that had meant so much to her that it had obscured all else, the sacrifices she'd been willing to make, the children she'd never had. The pursuit of perfection, and driving herself. Even the dog who had become a substitute child. And the compromises she hadn't made for John, because she had been too afraid to make room for him, not in her closets but in her heart. Because if she had given him everything, which she had anyway, she would have lost too much if she lost him, which she had. It was all there in the story, page after page, as December oozed into January. She was deep into it when Adrian arrived, and he thought she looked better, although still too thin and so pale she was almost gray. But she didn't leave her room for days. She was writing furiously. And he was still in Paris when the realtor called to say she had an apartment for her. In the Seventh Arrondissement, on the Boulevard de La Tour Maubourg. She called Adrian, who was staying at the Ritz too, as usual, and he promised to come and see it with her after the Gaultier show. She had been carefully avoiding all the people from the fashion world. She had nothing to say to them anymore.

She sneaked out of the hotel with him, wearing dark glasses with her hair pulled back, and a coat with a hood. It was pouring rain. But even in the rain, the apartment was beautiful. The house it was in was behind another building, on a cobbled courtyard, with a small meticulously kept garden. A couple who now lived in Hong Kong owned the house and were never there. They didn't have the heart to sell it and it was easy to see why. The apartment occupied the top floor and the attic, and it had a roof garden. It was just big enough for her and no one else. And there was a studio in the attic where she could write. She rented it on the spot, and they said she could move in right away. It was simply furnished with some antiques and a big canopied bed. It had lovely moldings and three-hundred-year-old wood floors. She could see herself there for a long time, and so could Adrian.

'It looks like Mimi's garret in *La Bohème*. And you're beginning to look like her too,' Adrian said with concern, but he was pleased for her. He could see her being happy there, and she told him about the book. She had no idea when she would finish it. She hoped it would be by spring at the rate she was going. But it didn't matter how long it took. She didn't even know if she would publish it, but writing it was doing her good.

As she signed the lease the next day, and wrote a check, she realized that it would have been her first wedding anniversary. She didn't know if it was some kind of omen, or an unhappy co-incidence, and she went back to the Ritz after that and got drunk on champagne with Adrian in her room. He was still worried about her, with good reason. She was drifting loose, and the more she drank, the more she talked about John that night, about forgiving him for what he'd done, and running out on her, that she understood and it was all right, and it didn't matter, and he'd been right, she'd been terrible to him. But not as terrible as she'd been to herself since, Adrian realized. She was still blaming herself, and he wondered if she missed her job, although she said she didn't, but he wasn't sure if he believed her. Her life seemed so empty to him now, so unpopulated except for the characters in her book. And more than anything, he knew, she needed to forgive her-self, and he wondered if she ever would, or if she would be haunted forever by the ghosts of what could have been. It still broke his heart to see her that way. And it made him furious with John for leaving her. Their life may have been chaotic, but she was a hell of a good woman. Adrian thought John had been a fool for leaving her, and running out of patience so soon.

Adrian hated to leave her, when he left Paris at the end of the week. She was moving into her apartment the next day, but he couldn't stay to help her. He had meetings in New York he had to get back to, one of them with John Anderson. *Chic* was having trouble with the agency, but he didn't tell Fiona that. It wasn't easy stepping into her shoes, and it was a challenge for him. He admired her more each day as he juggled a thousand balls in the air and prayed he could manage them. He had asked Fiona's advice on several things, and was impressed as always by her clear head, her fine mind, her infallible judgment, and her extraordinary taste. She was a remarkable woman, and he was sure the book would be good. She was putting her heart and soul into it. As Adrian flew out of Charles de Gaulle, he thought of her, as he always did, and prayed she would be safe. She seemed so vulnerable and so frail, and yet so strong at the same time. He admired her courage even more than he did her style.

As Adrian flew back to the States, Fiona was moving into the apartment on the Boulevard de La Tour Maubourg. The rooms were drafty, and the sky was gray, and she found a small leak in the kitchen, but the place was clean. It came with linens and dishes, and pots and pans. There were two bedrooms and two bathrooms, a tiny living room, a cozy kitchen where she could entertain friends, and the studio upstairs, which would be filled with sunlight on a good day. It was all she needed. For the first few days she missed the Ritz and the familiar faces there, the night maid who always checked on her, the telephone operator who recognized her voice, the doorman who tipped his hat to her, the baby-faced bellboys in the round blue caps who looked like little boys and carried packages to her, and the concierges who took care of all her minor secretarial needs. She never went anywhere, so she didn't need reservations, but they got things for her, mailed her letters and packages, had pages xeroxed, bought books she needed for research, and were always pleasant when she stopped at the desk to talk to them.

It was lonely in the apartment at first. She had no one to talk to. She couldn't order something to eat at any hour, but in some ways it was good for her. She had to get dressed and go out, even if it was only in jeans and an old sweater. There was a bistro around the corner where she ate once in a while, or had coffee, and a grocery store a few blocks away where she stocked up on food. Sometimes she holed up in the apartment until she ran out of cigarettes and food. She had started smoking again, which didn't help her weight. She was wasting away and her clothes hung on her, but all she wore anyway were sweatshirts and old sweaters and jeans. She felt very French when she smoked, sitting at some sidewalk café, reading the latest pages of her manuscript. And most of the time she was pleased.

It rained a lot in Paris that winter, and continued to do so as winter wended into spring. In April, when the sun finally came out, she took long walks along the quais. She stood looking at the Seine one day, and remembered her dinner with John on the Bateau Mouche. It was nearly two years ago, and she felt as though she had lived an entire lifetime since. The life she had lived then had vanished into thin air. The people, the job at *Chic*, even Sir Winston. And John of course. He seemed the furthest away of all, and was.

By May she was feeling better, and the book was going well. She smiled sometimes when she read the pages, and even laughed out loud sitting in her studio all by herself. She had led a solitary life in Paris for more than six months, but she realized now that it had done her good. She felt more like herself again when Adrian came back in June, and he was relieved to see her looking so well. She had gained a little weight, and was smoking like a chimney, but her color was good. She had cut her hair a little, her green eyes were bright and animated, and she looked great, even to him. He always had a critical eye about her, and she was still his dearest friend, even though she was living so far away. He liked what she told him about the book.

She was willing to go to Le Voltaire with him this time, and she was fine about it when they ran into another magazine editor. She had nothing to hide now. She no longer looked defeated and was doing well. And in answer to the question 'What are you doing now?' she answered with a smile that she was writing a book.

'Oh God, not a roman à clef, I hope,' the editor said, looking panicked, and Fiona laughed.

'I couldn't do that to my friends. I'm writing a novel, and there's nothing about the fashion industry in it, or the publishing world. Your secrets are safe with me.' The editor in question rolled her eyes and looked relieved. And then Fiona turned to Adrian with a grin after the woman left. 'Writing a book about fashion would bore the hell out of me.' They both laughed, and splurged on a gigantic plate of profiteroles for both of them for dessert. He was relieved to see her eating well, although she had smoked intermittently throughout the meal.

'What about getting another dog one of these days?' Adrian had been meaning to suggest it to her for a long time, but he had been waiting for the wound of losing Sir Winston to heal. It had been long enough now for him to risk suggesting it to her, but she lit another cigarette and shook her head.

'Remember me? I'm back to my old self again. No responsibilities, no attachments, no encumbrances. I don't want to own anything, love anyone, or get too attached to people, places, or things. It's a rule that seems to work well for me.' It told him that she was still wounded, and perhaps always would be. And the wound John had left, for however short a time he had been in her life, had been the worst of all. But Adrian had the sense that she had at least begun to forgive herself,

213

for whatever mistakes she'd made, and whatever she had been unable to give him. In her months of solitude, she had fought hard for deeper insights into herself. For the first time since she had left the magazine and moved to Paris, Adrian felt she had done the right thing. She was deeper and wiser, and more profound than she had been. Her life was less frivolous, there were no strange house men running around in harem pants. She was less fashionable, and less interested in fashion and the clothes she wore. She seemed less perfectionistic, and not as hard on herself. She seemed a lot more relaxed and more philosophical in many ways, and she said she enjoyed cleaning the apartment herself. But the one thing that worried him was that she was leading a lonely life, and she had isolated herself. At forty-four, she was still too young to shut herself out of the world. She said she had no interest in dating, and she didn't want a social life. All she wanted was to finish her book. She had set a goal to complete it by the end of the summer, and then she was going to come to New York briefly to find an agent, to sell it for her. She was staying in Paris for the summer so she could work, seemed to have no interest in going to the South of France, and almost recoiled when Adrian asked her if she was going to St. Tropez. It was obvious that he had hit a nerve. There were a lot of places she didn't want to go, or be anymore. She said she had no interest in them. But they both knew they just hurt too much.

He lingered for a few days after the couture shows to visit with her, and when he left Paris in early July, she got back to work. But it had been a nice interlude for her, seeing Adrian. They talked on the phone frequently, but it was better being face-to-face, and they had lunch at Le Voltaire almost every day. She cooked dinner for him in her apartment once, and they sat on her terrace eating cheese and drinking wine. He had to admit, she hadn't chosen a bad life, and in a way he envied her. Still, he was having a ball in her old job, and had made a number of dramatic changes since she left.

'Maybe I'll come to Paris and write a book when I grow up,' he said as he stretched his legs. He was wearing a fabulous pair of new Manolo python shoes.

'You should write the one I didn't write,' Fiona said with a smile. 'About the fashion world. You know more secrets than I do.' Everyone confided in Adrian, and he was as silent as a tomb. She always knew her own secrets were safe with him.

'They'd all put contracts out on me. Although if they haven't yet, maybe they never will.' He liked her idea, but in his life, it was still years away. He was in the same place she had been at his age.

Once he was gone, her book started to pick up speed, and she rarely took a break from it after that. She got up at dawn, made coffee, lit a cigarette, and sat down to work. And most of the time, she didn't look up from her computer till noon. She ate some fruit, stretched, and got back to work. She sat there day and night for two months. Paris was deserted in the summer, even the tourists seemed to go somewhere else, to Brittany or the South, or Italy or Spain. And she never left her apartment, except to buy food.

It was a brilliantly sunny day at the end of August when she wrote a sentence, and sat staring at it with tears in her eyes, realizing what had just happened. She had finished the book.

'Oh my God,' she said softly, and then gave a wild whoop of glee and started laughing and crying. 'Oh my God . . . I did it!!' She sat staring at it, and read the line over and over and over again. She had done it. The book she had put her heart and soul into was complete. It had taken her almost exactly eight months.

She called Adrian, it was morning for him, and he had just come to work. As soon as he heard it was Fiona, he picked up the phone.

'You can have your job back now,' he said, sounding exasperated. 'They're driving me nuts. Three of my best editors just quit.'

'You'll find others. They're all replaceable, including me. Guess what?' she said, chortling with excitement.

'You're pregnant. It's the immaculate conception. Or you've met a cute boy. You're moving back to New York, please God, and you want to work for me.'

'Not on your life. None of the above. I just

finished the book!' Her excitement flew right through the phone.

'Holy SHIT! I don't believe it! Already? You're a genius!' He was excited for her. He knew how much it meant to her. And as always, he was proud of her. They were each the brother and sister the other had never had. 'Are you coming home now?' he asked hopefully.

'This is home now. But I'll come to New York in a few weeks. I want to talk to some agents. I have to clean up the manuscript first. I want to make some changes and corrections.' And in the end, it took longer than she thought.

It was October before she was ready to come to New York. She had three agents to see, and she was going to stay with Adrian. She still had tenants at her place, and she had decided to sell her house. She was going to put it on the market while she was in town, and she was going to offer it to her tenants first. If they could make a deal, it would save them both real estate agents' fees, which might be good for both of them, and they loved the house. She had made a decision not to come back to New York to live. She was happy in Paris, and she had nothing in New York anymore. Except Adrian, and he didn't mind coming to Paris to see her. And as soon as she got back, she was going to start another book. She had already started the outline, and she worked on it some more on the plane.

Fiona met Adrian at the magazine, and it felt

strange to her, like visiting a childhood home where other people now lived. And it was even stranger, visiting her house. They had painted the rooms other colors, and filled it with furniture she thought was hideous, but it was theirs now, and no longer hers. And they were thrilled at the prospect of buying it. They settled on a mutually agreeable price within two days, avoided the agents' fees, and the trip had been worthwhile if only for that.

She and Adrian spent nights in his apartment, and she went to meet the literary agents she'd lined up. She strongly disliked two of them, but the third one she saw seemed just right. He was intelligent and ambitious, interesting to talk to, knew his business backward and forward, and was roughly her own age. She told him what the book was about, and he liked it. She left a manuscript with him, and she felt as though she were leaving her baby with strangers. She was a nervous wreck when she went back to Adrian's apartment that night. She had stayed with the agent for hours, and Adrian had dinner waiting for her. He knew how stressful it was for her meeting with agents about her book.

'What if he hates it?' she said, looking anxious. She had worn a white turtleneck and gray slacks, with gray satin loafers and her signature turquoise bracelet on her wrist. She hadn't even noticed it, but the agent had been very taken with her. All Fiona cared about was her book. She hadn't even worn make-up, she rarely did anymore, but her skin was so exquisite, and her eyes so huge, that Adrian thought she was actually prettier that way.

'He's not going to hate it. You write beautifully, Fiona. And the story is solid.' She had read him passages, faxed him pages, and gone over the outline with him, in its many mutations, a million times.

'He'll hate it. I know he will,' she said, emptying a glass of wine. She got a little drunk as they sat there, which was rare for her. And by the next morning, she had convinced herself that the agent would reject it, and was steeling herself to stick the manuscript in a drawer somewhere. She was already concentrating on the new book.

The phone rang at Adrian's late that afternoon. Fiona usually let the machine pick it up, but for some reason she answered it, thinking it might be Adrian. They were trying to connect for dinner that night, although he was even busier than she had been when she had his job. The only difference was that he didn't give parties, and never let photographers or models stay with him. But he had admitted to her a year before, when she left, that he had hired Jamal. And Fiona had been happy to see him when she arrived. Adrian had put him in a uniform, black pants and a white shirt, with a little white jacket he wore and a tie on the rare times when Adrian entertained. And Adrian said Jamal wasn't nearly as happy with him, because he couldn't get cast-offs from him, his shoes were too big. But Jamal seemed very happy in his new job.

'Hello?' Fiona said cautiously when she picked up the phone. The voice on the other end was unfamiliar. It wasn't Adrian, and she was sorry she had answered it. But much to her surprise, the voice asked for her. It was Andrew Page, the literary agent she had seen the day before.

He gave her the news fast and quick. He knew how anxious new authors were, and he told her almost instantly that he loved the book, it was one of the best first novels he had read in years. He thought she should do a little more editing, but not much, and he thought he already had a publisher for it. He was having lunch with a senior editor the next day on her behalf. If she was willing to sign with him, of course. He asked her to come in and sign a contract with him the next morning.

'Are you serious?' she almost screamed at him. 'Are you kidding?'

'Of course I'm not kidding,' he laughed. For a woman of such power and capability, she was amazingly humble about her writing, and most other things, and he liked that about her. 'It's a terrific book.'

'And you are a fabulous agent!' she said, laughing. They made an appointment for the next day, and she hung up, and two minutes later, she called Adrian on his cell phone. 'Guess what?'

'Not that again.' He laughed at her. She loved

making him guess whatever fantastic thing had just happened, just like a little kid. And she sounded like one on the phone. He knew it had to be good.

'Andrew Page loved my book! I'm signing with him tomorrow. And he's having lunch with a senior editor about it.' She sounded as if she had just given birth to twins, and in a way she had. She had also told him about the new book, and he was going to try and get her a two- or three-book contract. Publishers liked knowing it wasn't going to be a book from a onetime author. And that she clearly wasn't.

'Am I supposed to be surprised?' Adrian asked, sounding blasé. 'I told you he'd love the book.' She had started on a whole new career. 'Next, he's going to be selling it for a movie, and we'll all go to Hollywood for the premiere. And if you write the screenplay, I want to be your escort when you accept the Oscar.'

'I love you, and thank you for the vote of confidence, but you're nuts. Now you have to have dinner with me tonight so we can celebrate. Can you do it?' He was still trying to get out of a previous engagement, but he promised her he would. He wanted to take her out and fuss over her a bit. They agreed to meet at eight o'clock at La Goulue, which was still her favorite restaurant in New York.

And when she got in a cab to meet him, she was wearing the only slightly dressy dress she had

221

brought with her. It was a little vintage black cocktail dress by Dior that she had bought at Didier Ludot in the Palais Royal. It looked spectacular on her. She was wearing her hair down, and it shone like burnished copper, and in honor of her new career as a soon-to-be author, she had even deigned to wear make-up. The dress was short and showed off her legs, and she was wearing astonishingly high Manolo Blahnik sandals with ankle straps that nearly made Jamal drool. She looked more than a little bit like Audrey Hepburn in *Breakfast at Tiffany's*, except for the bright red hair.

The headwaiter at La Goulue was thrilled to see her, they spoke in French and he complained that he hadn't seen her in a year. She explained that she had moved to Paris, and as he led her to a corner table on the banquette, heads turned. Fiona looked more spectacular than ever. She was about to sit down, when a familiar face caught her eye. Ordinarily, she wouldn't have said hello to him, it seemed easier not to. But as he was only two tables away from hers, it was just too rude. It was John.

She stopped and smiled at him, but it was not a greeting of seduction, it was a bittersweet one in recognition of old times. She noticed that the woman with him was very respectable looking and very blond. She looked almost as though she could have been his late wife's twin. And she was the head of the local Junior League. They had been dating for six months, and had the comfortable air of people who knew each other well.

John looked more than a little startled for a moment, in fact he looked thunderstruck and uncomfortable, and then graciously stood up, acknowledged Fiona, and politely introduced her to his date. He looked supremely ill at ease as the two women shook hands.

'Elizabeth Williams, Fiona Monaghan.' The two women checked each other out, and there was instant recognition in the eyes of the blonde. She had obviously heard about Fiona, and she looked slightly discomfited by the long red hair and good legs. Fiona looked like a model, and ten years younger than she was. She was the kind of woman who would have made any other woman nervous, knowing the man she was involved with had slept with her, or worse yet been in love with her. But John had left her after all, not the reverse. So he was not carrying a torch for her, as far as Fiona was concerned.

'Nice to see you, John,' Fiona said pleasantly, after acknowledging the woman he was having dinner with. She hadn't paid much attention to her name. More than anything, she was a type, and exactly whom Fiona would have expected to see with John. She was precisely who and what Fiona had predicted he would end up with, and apparently he had. And he looked well. She suddenly wanted to tell him about her book and her new agent, but it seemed a little foolish doing so, so she refrained.

'How've you been?' he asked, as though they had been old tennis partners that had drifted out of sight in the last year, or as though the only contact they had ever had was through their work.

'Wonderful. I'm living in Paris,' she said, but even after not seeing him for a year, or being in his life for longer than that, she could feel her heart begin to pound. Much to her chagrin, even after all this time, the magic wasn't gone. She wasn't healed. But he clearly was. He knew she had left the magazine, and thought she had gone to Paris for a few months, he didn't realize she had actually moved. 'I just sold my house,' and wrote a book! she nearly screamed. But she was demure and reserved. He nodded, and without saying more, she moved on and sat down. She hoped Adrian would come soon.

As luck would have it, it took him another half an hour to get there, and she was ready to have a nervous breakdown by the time he arrived, although she looked sophisticated, poised, and cool, as she made some notes on a pad, and never even glanced at John. She forced herself to look at ease and unconcerned.

'Did you see who's sitting there?' she whispered to Adrian through clenched teeth, as he sat across from her, with his back to John.

'Is it someone fabulous?' he asked, as she warned him not to turn around and look.

'Used to be,' she whispered. 'It's John. He's with

224

some blond debutante, who looked like she wanted to kill me.'

'He's with a young girl?' Adrian looked surprised, that had never seemed to be John's thing.

'No, she's older than I am, I think. Just that type.'

'Are you okay?' he asked solicitously.

'No.' She felt as if she were about to cry, but she would have died first, and she felt sick. 'This is hard.' She had used every ounce of control and discipline she had to maintain the charade of indifference until Adrian arrived.

'I know it is.' She had given up a life, a job, a city, a house, and a country over him, just to get over him. Seeing him again was bound to be a bitch. 'Do you want to leave?' Adrian whispered sympathetically. He wouldn't blame her if she did.

'I'll look like a fool . . . or a wimp . . .' She fought back tears, but no one would have guessed it in a million years.

'Okay. Then sit there and smile. Laugh your ass off. Pretend I'm amusing you to death. Come on . . . that's it . . . give me some teeth, Fiona . . . more . . . I want you to pretend that you've never been happier in your life.' He was right.

'What if I throw up?'

'I'll kill you if you do. Where did you get that dress, by the way? It's to die for.' Leave it to Adrian to notice her dress at a time like this. She smiled genuinely as she answered.

'Didier Ludot. It's vintage Dior couture, from the sixties. It barely covers my ass.'

'Good. I hope he got a good look, and feels as sick as you do, over what he gave up.' As he said it, Fiona looked surprised.

'I thought you thought it was all my fault, because of the compromises and adjustments I didn't make.'

'I never said that,' Adrian corrected her, and she looked incensed.

'Yes, you did.'

'I'm your friend, Fiona. I tell you when I think you're wrong. That's what friends do. I'm always honest with you. So I told you I thought you should adjust to him. But I think he is a chicken-shit sonofabitch for throwing in the towel and walking out in a matter of months. You should have done a lot of things differently, and could have if you wanted to, like empty your closets for him, and keep the chaos to a minimum. But he should have kicked his kids' asses, fired his housekeeper, and killed his dog, and stuck with the greatest woman that ever lived. He was a damn fool.' Fiona looked stunned and pleased. He had never told her how sorry he felt for her, or how angry he was at John. She had been in such bad shape, he had tried to underplay the damage to her, and minimize it, so she would have the guts to get back on her feet. He had always feared that too much sympathy would give her permission to fall apart and stay that way.

Instead, she pulled herself together remarkably.

'You really think so?' She felt vindicated finally, and wished he had told her before. His respect made a huge difference to her, as much as his empathy.

'Of course I do. You weren't the only one to blame. You were silly, and even stupid at times, and you should have given me Jamal then. A guy like John can't deal with eccentric bullshit like that. You needed to be less Holly Golightly and more Audrey Hepburn, and you look like her in that dress by the way.' He could afford to be honest with her now. She was fine. Better than fine. She was great, even if the wounds still hurt. But she had survived.

'Which one do I look like?' she teased, but she liked what he had just said.

'Miss Hepburn, of course.'

'I always thought that you thought it was all my fault.'

'Of course not. He damn near destroyed your life, for chrissake. First he talks you into marrying him, and then he dumps you, because you have a crazy house man, too many clothes in your closets, and his kids are two raving bitches. A lot of that, maybe even most of it, wasn't your fault. I think you were just too much for him, Fiona. You scared him to death.' They both knew that was true.

'Yeah, I think I did. And he made a deal with his girls.'

'That sucks. You can't let kids blackmail you

into giving up someone you love. He fell in love with who you are, in all your glory, and then he ran like a scared rabbit because you weren't Heidi. Please. The guy has no balls.' Adrian looked annoyed, and Fiona laughed.

'I guess that tells it like it is.' He was making this chance meeting with John much easier for her. And she was looking more relaxed by the minute. She was almost glowing. And John saw it. Or at least Adrian hoped so.

'He should have stuck it out and worked it out. Speaking of which, now that you're about to become a famous author, what are you going to do about your life?'

'What life?' She looked blank. She had almost forgotten that John was sitting two tables away with the WASP of his dreams.

'That's exactly my point. You don't have a life. You're too young to give it all up. Look at you, you're the best-looking woman in this restaurant. You don't need to be the editor of *Chic* magazine to have a life. You have to start getting out.'

'You mean like dating? No way.' She looked horrified at the thought.

'Don't give me that,' Adrian scolded her. 'You need to meet people in Paris. Go to dinner. Have lunch. Never mind dating, if you're not ready. But for chrissake, once in a while at least, leave your house.'

'Why? I'm happy writing.' And she was about to start another book.

'You're wasting your life, and you'll be sorry when you get old. You're not going to look like that forever. Go out and have some fun. Otherwise, why live in Paris?'

'I can smoke.'

'I'm going to come over and drag you out, if you don't do something about it soon. You're becoming a recluse.'

'No, I already am one,' she said, looking confident and incredibly glamorous. There was something about Fiona that no other woman had, and from where he sat two tables away, John had seen it too. She had guts, panache, and style, along with looks that took his breath away. And Elizabeth Williams was not pleased. John had been trying not to look at Fiona since she sat down, but her pull was more powerful than he was, he kept glancing at her. She looked like she was having a terrific time. She had never looked at him once since she sat down.

'You never told me she was that beautiful,' Elizabeth said plaintively, 'and so young. I thought you said she was in her forties.'

'She is. She just looks good for her age. Looking good is her business. She runs a fashion magazine, or she used to.' He had always wondered why she quit. He had heard rumors of health problems, and had no idea if it was true. She looked healthy enough to him. He wondered if she just got bored with her job. The coincidence of timing had never occurred to him. Sometimes men just weren't very

229

smart about things like that. It never dawned on John that she had quit her job because of him.

'She's a very pretty girl,' Elizabeth conceded through clenched teeth, and then went on to complain about all the problems she was having with the Junior League fashion show. Anyone but Elizabeth would have realized that John looked bored. She loved to hear herself talk.

Much to Fiona's relief, as the food she and Adrian had ordered was set down in front of them, John paid for the dinner he and Elizabeth had eaten, and without looking at her, they got up and left. It was only once they were on the sidewalk, trying to decide whether to go to her place or his, that he glanced back into the restaurant through the open picture windows and saw Fiona laughing and talking to Adrian. And just as Adrian had, he noticed the striking resemblance to Audrey Hepburn. His eyes were riveted to her, but Elizabeth didn't notice. She was complaining about her twenty-year-old daughter and fourteen-year-old son. She was a widow, and had been nagging John to spend time with them, and he was hesitant to do so. He didn't want to mislead her kids, and he was not yet sure how committed he was to their mother. It had taken him time to get over Fiona. And he was sure he had. Until tonight. He had almost forgotten how beautiful she was, and how just seeing her could turn him upside down. Without meaning to, or knowing it, she was doing it to him again.

'You're not listening to me,' Elizabeth complained, as John dragged his attention back to her. 'You haven't listened to me all night.' He hadn't heard a word she said since Fiona walked into the restaurant.

'I'm sorry. I was thinking of something else.'

'I said, why don't we go to your place? My kids are at mine.'

'I'm sorry, Elizabeth. I've had an incredible headache all day. Would you mind terribly if I drop you off at home?' He wanted to go home and be alone with his thoughts. He wasn't in the mood to make love to her tonight. Sometimes just being with her was an incredible drain. And there wasn't anything she could say about it if he wasn't feeling well. She couldn't insist that he take her to bed. He dropped her off at her place a few minutes later, and went back to his own apartment in a cab.

Fiona and Adrian were finishing dinner by then, and they went back to his apartment, and talked about Andrew Page. She couldn't wait to hear how his lunch with the editor went the next day. If nothing else, thinking about her book kept her mind off John.

14

Fiona signed the contract with Andrew Page the next day, and in the late afternoon he called her on her cell phone. The lunch had gone well, and the editor had agreed to read her book. She'd been excited about it when Andrew described it to her, and she was impressed that Fiona was the author. She knew who she was. She thought Fiona would be fabulous to publicize a book, and there was no question that that was part of the package they had to sell. Looks and style weren't everything, but they certainly helped.

By the end of the week, Fiona had accomplished all she'd gone to New York to do. She had sold her house, spent time with Adrian, found an agent, and a major publishing house was considering her book. Andrew had sent the manuscript to the editor the next day. Fiona had even run into John. It hadn't been easy for her, but she had dealt with it. It was bound to happen one day. She wasn't entirely over him, but she had made progress and was on her way. Now she was anxious to get back to Paris and start her new book. She was going to do some more work on the outline on the plane.

Adrian had promised to spend Christmas in Paris with her that year. And when she went back she was going to make a serious effort to find a house she could buy. Fiona had left her things in storage in New York, but she was getting anxious to see them again. The apartment she was in suited her, but she wanted something permanent. Fiona knew for sure now that she was not moving back to New York. It was hard to believe she had been gone a year. And she was relieved to find that she no longer missed her job. She had at first, but she was feeling encouraged about her writing. It was fulfilling a dream for her. Even though other dreams had died.

Within a week of her return, Fiona had seen two houses she didn't like, and started her new book. She was off and running, and by Thanksgiving, she had made a good start. They had heard from the editor by then, who had declined her book. She felt it was too serious for them, and somewhat cumbersome. But Andrew wasn't discouraged, and told her not to be. He had already sent it to someone else.

On Thanksgiving morning, Adrian called. He was up at five A.M., starting to stuff and cook his turkeys. He was having thirty people over for dinner, and said he was going insane.

'I feel like a gynecologist. I just stuffed five birds.'

'You're disgusting.' She laughed at him.

'And what are you doing today?'

'Nothing. It isn't a holiday here. I'm working on my book.'

'That's sacrilegious,' he chided her. 'Then what are you grateful for?' It was a good question, and good to be reminded that she had much to be grateful for, even if things hadn't worked out as she'd planned.

'You,' she said without hesitating. 'And my work.' She was grateful that she had finished one book and started a second.

'And that's it? That's a pathetic list.'

'It's enough,' she said peacefully. She still hadn't done anything about her social life, and she didn't really care. 'I can't wait to see you in a few weeks,' she said happily. He was coming over for Christmas, and they were busy making plans. He was going to stay with her, as she had with him in New York. He was going to stay in her guest room, and they had agreed to go to Chartres, since he'd never been. And he'd be back again in January for the haute couture. She loved knowing she was going to see him twice in the next two months. He was still the best friend she had.

She wished him luck with his dinner, wished him a Happy Thanksgiving, got nostalgic for a minute, and then reminded herself that there was no point. She had better things to do than feel sorry for herself, although she felt homesick when she thought of the dinner he was giving and wished she could be there.

She had just started writing again, when the telephone rang. She thought it might be Adrian again, asking her advice about his birds. It was rare for anyone to call her, sometimes she didn't speak to anyone for days. And she had spoken to Andrew Page the day before. No one other than Andrew and Adrian ever called her, and her agent wouldn't call her on Thanksgiving.

'Why are you calling me? I can't cook,' she said, expecting to hear Adrian's voice, and was startled when it wasn't. It was a familiar voice, but she couldn't place it for a moment. And then her heart gave a lurch as she did. It was John.

'That's quite an admission. The truth comes out. You always told me you could.'

'Sorry,' she said skittishly, 'I thought it was Adrian. He's cooking Thanksgiving dinner in New York.' She had no idea where John was calling her from, and wasn't sure she cared. She did, of course, but she wasn't going to let herself care anymore. She had promised herself that again in New York. It was strange that he had called. He had never called her since he left. All their communications, what there were of them, had been through their lawyers. She lapsed into silence while she waited to hear why he'd called.

'I was just doing some business in London, and I stopped in Paris on the way home,' he explained. 'I just had a crazy thought. It's Thanksgiving, and

I wondered if you wanted to have lunch or dinner with me at Le Voltaire.' He knew it was her favorite restaurant, and he had liked it too when they'd been there together. He sounded awkward as he asked. And there was a long, long pause at her end of the phone.

'Why?' She said the single word. What was the point?

'Old times' sake, or something like that. Maybe we can be friends.' But she didn't want to be his friend. She had been in love with him, and still was. She knew that when she saw him in New York. And he had found a woman who looked just like Ann.

'I'm not sure I need a friend,' Fiona said bluntly. 'I don't know how these things work. I've never been divorced before. I'm an amateur at all this. Are we supposed to be friends?'

'If we want to be,' he said cautiously, although he felt awkward answering her. 'I'd like to be your friend, Fiona. I thought what we had was special. It just didn't work out.' Apparently not, since he had left her in less than six months and he was still trying to justify it to her. She remembered what Adrian had said, that he thought it was lousy of him to walk out on her, and it hadn't all been her fault. She had felt better about herself after Adrian said it.

'I'm not mad at you,' she said honestly. 'I think I'm just hurt.' Very, very, very hurt. It was a mild understatement. In the early months, she had thought about whether she could go on living, instead she had quit her job, given up her career, and her house, and moved to Paris. Hurt didn't even begin to describe it. But in the end, things had worked out. She had a new career, and with luck, she would sell a book.

'I know,' John said sadly, in response to Fiona saying she'd been hurt. 'I feel very guilty about it.' As well he should.

'That's appropriate.' She didn't tell him that Adrian thought so too.

'I just didn't know how to deal with your life. We were so different. Too different.' He tried to explain, and she cut him off. She didn't want to hear it again. It was all done.

'I think we've covered all that. How's your friend?'

'What friend?' He was drawing a blank.

'The Junior League lady I saw you with at La Goulue.'

He sounded stunned. 'How did you know she's with the Junior League? Do you know each other?' Elizabeth hadn't said they did, and he sounded surprised.

'No. She just looks it. It's written all over her. She looks like Ann.'

'Yes, she does.' And then he laughed and decided to be honest with her. It was a small step toward friendship, which was what he had told himself he wanted when he called her. 'To tell the truth, she bores me.'

'Oh. I'm sorry.' Fiona hated herself for it, but she was glad to hear it. 'She's nice looking.'

'So are you. You looked fabulous at La Goulue. Paris agrees with you. What are you doing here?'

'Writing. Novels. I finished a book this summer, and I just started another. It's fun. I like it. I was in New York to find an agent.'

'And did you?' He was interested. Everything about her had always intrigued him. He still thought she was amazing, and this proved it. She had given up one of the most successful careers in New York, moved to Paris, and started another. And he was sure, knowing her, that her book would be a best-seller.

'I signed with Andrew Page.'

'That's impressive. Has he sold anything yet?'

'No, but I got my first rejection. So I guess now I'm officially a writer.' She suspected there would be lots more of them, but Andrew seemed confident that he could sell her work, so she wasn't worried.

'Why don't we talk about it at lunch? If we stay on the phone long enough, there won't be anything left to say.' She wasn't sure there was anyway. 'Will you meet me at Le Voltaire, or somewhere else if you prefer?' He sounded more confident than he felt, and she was annoyed. Why was he calling her? What was the point? It was over. And she didn't need or want his friendship. She hesitated for a long time as she mulled it over, and he got worried. 'Come on, Fiona. Please. I miss talking to you. I'm not going to hurt you.' He didn't have to. He already had. Far too much. She thought she had forgiven him, but now she was beginning to wonder.

'I can't stay long,' she said finally, and he exhaled slowly at his end. 'I have to get back to work. It's hard to start again once I'm interrupted.'

'It's Thanksgiving. We can order turkey or chicken or something. Or profiteroles.' He had remembered her fatal weakness for them. There was a lot he remembered about her. Most of it good. It was only rarely now that he remembered the bad. And it no longer seemed quite so important. A lot of it seemed silly to him. Like the closets. The crazy people she knew and loved. And Jamal, running around in sarongs and her gold sandals. 'What time will you meet me?'

'One o'clock,' she said in a flat voice, feeling foolish for letting him talk her into it. There was something very persuasive about him. And she had always loved his voice.

'Should I pick you up? I'm at the Crillon, and I have a car.' She didn't, but it was none of his business. She could walk from where she was.

'I'll meet you there.'

'I'll have the concierge reserve a table. Thanks for coming to lunch. It'll be good to see you.' He still had the vision of her he had had ever since he'd seen her at La Goulue. And Elizabeth had mentioned her several times. She was a fearsome opponent, and a tough act to follow.

Fiona stood staring at herself in the mirror after she hung up. She was sorry she had agreed to meet him. She was tired, her hair was dirty, and she had dark circles under her eyes from writing into the wee hours. But no matter how she looked, she didn't want to see him, she told herself, and then groaned, as she realized she did. She flew into action then, washed her hair, took a bath, shaved her legs for no particular reason, and dug through her closet for a decent dress. In the end, she settled on black leather pants, a white T-shirt, and a mink sweater that Adrian loved. She had gotten the sweater at Didier Ludot too, it was the most famous vintage store in Paris, and she shopped there regularly, and had bought a collection of vintage Hermès bags. She pulled out one of them, a large red crocodile Kelly bag, and pulled out flats to match.

By the time she got to Le Voltaire, she was a nervous wreck. She didn't know why she'd agreed to meet him. She had worn her hair in a single long braid down her back. She had no idea how beautiful she looked when she walked in, slightly breathless, with a halo of soft hair that had gotten loose and framed her face, and the big green eyes he still thought of often. The black leather pants molded her body and reminded him of everything he'd missed. All he could think of now, as he looked at her, was what a fool he had been.

'Sorry I'm late,' she apologized. 'I walked.'

'You're not,' he reassured her. 'Where do you

live?' he asked as the maître d' led them to the corner booth that she and Adrian loved. John had gotten her number from information, but he didn't have her address.

'In the Seventh,' she said vaguely. 'I found a great apartment. Now I'm looking to buy a house.'

'You're staying?' he asked with a look of interest. She nodded as they sat down. And then he looked across the table at her and smiled. She looked as beautiful as he remembered, but more vulnerable and more accessible than she had in New York. She looked more glamorous there in her sexy black cocktail dress. Here she somehow looked younger and more real. 'So how does Sir Winston like Paris?' he asked with a gentle smile, as Fiona looked away.

'He died a year ago,' she said bluntly, and picked up the menu to distract herself so she didn't cry.

'Oh my God.' John looked crushed. He wanted to ask her what had happened, but he didn't dare. 'I'm so sorry. I know how much he meant to you.' She had had him for fifteen years when he died. 'Did you get another dog?'

'Nope,' she said simply, looking at him again. 'I get too attached. It's not a good idea.' He sensed correctly that she was referring to him too. Their brief marriage had cost her a great deal, even more than it had him. He could see it in her eyes. The pain he still saw there went straight to his heart.

'You should get a French bulldog. It would suit you.'

'I don't want one. No more dogs. Besides, they're too much work.' She tried to sound hard about it, but only succeeded in sounding sad. And he continued to have the impression they were really talking about him. 'So what are we going to eat?'

'Do they have a Thanksgiving menu?' he teased her, but he still felt terrible about the dog. Sir Winston must have died shortly after he left her. And he knew it must have been a terrible blow added to his own.

They settled on the shaved mushroom salad she always had, and she was torn between liver and blood sausage as he made a terrible face and she laughed.

'That's a hell of a thing to eat on Thanksgiving. You should at least have some kind of bird.' In the end she decided on veal, and he had the steak tartare. They agreed to share *pommes frites*, which he knew were delicious there. And then he asked her about her book.

They talked about it for an hour, and it sounded fascinating to him. 'May I borrow a manuscript? I'd really love to read it.'

'I don't have any spares.' She was still being cautious about him, but she had opened up a lot about the book. He could hear from her description of it how deeply she had delved into herself to do it and how painful it must have been.

'I'll give you a copy of it when it comes out, if it ever does.'

'What's the new one about?' They spent another hour talking about that. And by then they were sharing profiteroles.

'How long are you here?' she asked, as she ate the last of the delicious chocolate confection, looking like a little kid. He knew how she loved chocolate, and she ate more when the waiter brought them the little chocolate-covered coffee beans they always served at the end of the meal.

'Just two days. I spent a few days in London, and I have business here tomorrow. I'm going home on Saturday. My offer for dinner still stands if I behaved myself at lunch to your satisfaction.' She smiled at what he said.

'You did okay,' she conceded. 'I didn't want to come.'

'I know. I figured that out on the phone. I'm glad you did,' he said gently. 'I'm sorry about what happened. I was a real shit.' She was amazed by his honesty. It vindicated her in a way.

'Yes, you were a shit. But I did a lot of stupid stuff too. The photographer having an orgy with his drug dealer in the living room was definitely a low point in my career. I'm sorry that happened, and a lot of other dumb things. You'll be happy to know I gave away most of my clothes when I moved. I don't know why I was so possessive about my closets. I think I was obsessed with my wardrobe. It's a lot simpler here. I brought almost nothing.' Although she had bought quite a bit, mostly at Didier Ludot. 'My life is a lot simpler these days in a lot of ways. I want to keep it that way.' She sounded firm.

'Like what?' He was curious about her now. She seemed different somehow. Both more fragile and stronger, and deeper, and quieter. As though she had suffered a lot and come out the other end. Most of it thanks to him, he knew. But she had faced some old demons too, like her father's abandonment, her mother's death, the agonies of her childhood, and a stepfather who had raped her, although she had never told anyone except her therapist, not even John. It was all in the book. She had spent a number of years in therapy over the incident with her stepfather and made her peace with it long ago.

'I stripped a lot of deadwood out of my life,' she said simply. 'People, clothes, objects, possessions. A lot of stuff I didn't care about, or didn't need, and thought I did. It makes life a lot simpler. And cleaner somehow.' And then she looked at him. 'I'm sorry I did such a lousy job with your kids.'

'You didn't do anything wrong, Fiona. They were awful to you. I should have handled it better than I did. I didn't know what to do, so I ran.'

'I should have tried harder with them. I didn't know how either. I'm not very good with kids. It's a good thing I never had any of my own.'

'Do you regret that?'

'No, I don't. I think I would have been lousy at

it. My own childhood was too screwed up. The only thing I regret is not making it work with you. It's probably the most glaring failure of my life. I was too wrapped up in a lot of meaningless bullshit, like my own importance, and how I wanted to do things, and my job. I guess I was riding high on a wave, and thought I was hot shit. And then I got cut down to size.' He liked the size she was now. In a lot of ways. But he had liked her then too. She had knocked him right off his feet, and still could with very little effort. But she was being careful not to do that. She had no concept of the effect she had on him. She was too busy resisting what she still felt for him.

'Do you miss your job?' He was curious about that.

'No, I don't. I think I had pretty much done it. It was time to move on. And Adrian is doing a fabulous job.' But so had she. 'I had a good run. And now I love writing my books.' There was nothing she couldn't do, or so he thought.

'I'd love to see your apartment,' John said out of the blue as he paid the check, and Fiona looked up at him as though she had been struck by lightning.

'Why?' She looked terrified.

'Relax. Just curiosity. You have great taste. It's probably terrific, knowing you.'

'It's very small,' she said, looking guarded. She had let him in far enough. 'But I like it. It suits me. I'm not even sure I want to move, but I think I do. I wish the owners would sell me the whole house.

They live in Hong Kong and they're never here.' She was trying to get her realtor to look into it, and they had written them a letter, but she hadn't heard anything yet. The location was perfect and the house was adorable. She was willing to buy it if she could.

He had a car and driver outside, and the afternoon had gotten cold. She shivered in the wind despite her mink sweater, and he turned to her with a cautious smile. He had loved having lunch with her. And in some ways, she was glad she had. It had been nice to apologize to each other, and admit how wrong they had each been about some things. Maybe he was right, and they could be friends, although she wasn't entirely sure yet. She wanted to think about it.

'Can I give you a lift?' he offered, and she hesitated, and then nodded. She got in next to him and gave the driver her address.

He was impressed when he saw the building on the street. It was an imposing eighteenth-century hôtel particulier, but the real gem was in the court-yard behind it, where she lived. She explained it to him as she pointed to the rooftop. You could just barely see her house in the back. And then with a cautious look she asked him if he wanted to come up.

'Just for a minute. I have to get back to work,' she said precisely. And he nodded.

He followed her through the huge door in the front building, through which horse-drawn carriages had once passed, and walked into a courtyard that seemed magical to him. It was so typical of Fiona to have found it. And the house she lived in was as cute as she had said. She used her key and the code, turned off the alarm, and he followed her up the slightly crooked stairs, and a moment later they were in her apartment, and as he had suspected, it was lovely, and beautifully decorated. She had filled it with orchids, hung some paintings, and bought a few pieces of furniture herself. The entire effect was one of coziness and warmth, with her own inimitable brand of exotic chic. It was totally Fiona. She walked him up another flight of stairs to the studio with the roof garden where she worked, and he grinned broadly when he saw it.

'This is so you. I love it.' He would have loved to sit down and have a cup of tea, but she didn't invite him to. She seemed anxious for him to go. They had been together long enough. She needed to catch her breath. And sensing that, a moment later he left.

It took her hours to get back into her work. She was haunted by their lunch at Le Voltaire. And thinking of it kept distracting her. She kept hearing the things he had said. Walking along the Seine, and then later down the Faubourg St. Honoré, he was doing the same. He could see her face, hear her voice, and smell her perfume. She still dazzled him in just the way she once had, perhaps more so now that she seemed to have grown up. He liked who she had become, although at great price. But he felt less guilty now than he had before. He somehow felt as though they had both landed in a better place. And he loved the apartment where she lived.

He called her that night, but she didn't answer her phone. He suspected she was there, when he spoke to the machine. She was listening to him, and wondering why he had called. He thanked her for letting him come up to see her place. And the next day, wanting only to be polite, she called and thanked him for lunch.

'What about dinner tonight?' he suggested, as he had the day before, and she looked unhappy as she shook her head.

'I don't think it's a good idea.' She sounded stiff.

'Why not?' he asked sadly. He wanted to see her. He suddenly missed her more than he had in the past year, and he had the ghastly feeling that he had let a priceless diamond slip through his fingers. He had, and in her own way so had she. But she was willing to live with the loss. She had adjusted to it, and she had no desire to reopen old wounds. One thing she knew, and had always believed, no matter how many regrets you had, you could never go back. And she said as much to him. 'I wasn't suggesting we go back. I was suggesting that we move forward. If nothing else, we can be friends.'

'I'm not sure I can. It makes me too sad. It's like

looking at pictures of Sir Winston. I can't do that either. It hurts too much.'

'I'm sorry to hear it,' he said regretfully. He had a business meeting to go to then, and couldn't linger on the phone with her. He promised to call her later, but before he did, an enormous bouquet arrived for her from Lachaume. It was the most spectacular thing she had ever seen, and it embarrassed and worried her. She didn't want to start something with him. She left him a voice message thanking him at the hotel, knowing he was out, so she didn't have to speak to him again. And when he called her, she didn't pick up the phone. She let him talk to her machine. He was asking about dinner again that night. He suggested Alain Ducasse, or something comparable, or something simpler if she preferred. She never called him back, and stayed at her desk until late that night. She was still at her desk, in blue jeans and an old sweater, when she heard the bell. She couldn't imagine who it was, and she answered the intercom from her studio.

'*Qui est-ce?*' she asked in French.

'*Moi,*' said a familiar voice. It was eleven o'clock.

'What are you doing here?' It was John.

'I brought you dinner. I figured you didn't eat. Can I bring it up?' She wasn't sure whether to laugh or cry. Reluctantly, she buzzed him in and went to open her front door. He was standing there with some kind of box in a paper bag.

'You shouldn't be doing this,' she said, frowning at him, and trying to look stern. It was a look that had terrified junior editors for years, but he knew her better, and it didn't scare him. She took the bag into the kitchen, and when she opened it, she saw that it was profiteroles from Le Voltaire, and she turned to him with a smile. 'This is like my drug dealer showing up at the door.'

'I figured you needed the energy, or the calories, or something.' It was nice of him, but she didn't want to be tempted by him again. Profiteroles. Flowers. Lunch. He was like a man on a mission, or a quest. And she didn't want to be his prize.

'Do you want some?' she asked, putting the profiteroles on a plate. In spite of her reservations, she couldn't resist what he'd brought, and handed him a spoon as she sat down at her kitchen table, and he sat down next to her. And he ate one of them too. 'I don't want to get in a mess with you,' she said honestly. 'You broke my heart once. That was enough.' It was a calm clear statement that struck him like a blow.

'I know. I go a little nuts every time I'm around you, Fiona.' It was a classic understatement. He had been more than nuts when he left.

'I've been trying to stay away from you. It's better for both of us.'

'I'm not sure it is,' he said, equally honest with her. They always had been with each other, and she liked that about them. Or she had. 'Maybe we need to get this out of our system.'

She shook her head, with chocolate on her upper lip, which made him smile. He wished he could lick it off. 'We already did. It's out of our system. Let's keep it that way. For both our sakes. We don't need to destroy each other's lives again. We did that once.'

'What if it worked this time?' he said hopefully, wanting to convince her, and at the same time scared to death himself.

'What if it didn't? We'd both get hurt. Way too much.' It was like her decision about dogs. She didn't want one anymore. She didn't want to care that much. And she didn't want him either. She did, of course, but she didn't want the pain that would inevitably go with it, or his kids, or his housekeeper, or his insanely aggressive dog. But she didn't say all that to him. 'Besides, your kids would go nuts again.'

'They're a little older now. And I know better. Mrs. Westerman retired to North Dakota. She was a huge influence on them. And we could always put Fifi down. How's your ankle, by the way? No permanent damage, I hope.' Fiona laughed at the thought.

'She's one hell of a dog.'

'The dog from hell,' he corrected her, and she laughed again. 'She's living with Hilary at Brown. They let them have dogs. Maybe Fifi will get an education and shape up.'

'Do you want a glass of wine or something?' she offered, and he hesitated, looking apologetic. He had intruded on her and he knew it, but he didn't want to miss this opportunity, as long as he was in Paris.

'Am I keeping you from your work?'

'Yes, but you've already done it. I'm too tired now anyway. And the profiteroles make me lazy. Do you want a glass of port?' She still remembered how much he liked it, but he decided this time on a glass of white wine, and she poured one for him, and another for herself.

They settled in her small living room, John lit a fire in the fireplace, and they talked again about her book, his work, the new apartment he wanted to buy in New York, they rolled from one subject to another, and the companionship they shared warmed both their hearts. He was still talking about a house he had seen and fallen in love with on Cape Cod, when she leaned over to pour him another glass of wine, and he gently reached out and touched her face.

'I love you, Fiona,' he whispered in the light from the fire. She was more beautiful than ever in her old sweater, with her hair in an unruly braid.

'I love you, too,' she whispered back, 'but it doesn't matter anymore.' The moment had passed for them. But just as she thought it, he kissed her, and pulled her down next to him, and before she could object or even think about it, she was kissing him. It was just what she hadn't wanted to do, but she no longer remembered that, as a year's hunger for each other overtook them both, and it seemed like only moments later when they wound up in her bed. And they were both overwhelmed by such passion for each other that it was hours later when they stopped and caught their breath. She was half asleep by then.

'This was a terrible idea,' she whispered into his chest as she drifted off to sleep in his arms and he smiled down at her.

'No, it wasn't, it was the best idea we ever had,' he said, drifting off to sleep himself.

And when she awoke in the morning, wondering if it had been a dream, she stared at him in disbelief. 'Oh my God,' she said, looking at him. He was already awake, lying there holding her, and looking very pleased with himself. 'I can't believe we did that,' she said, looking mortified. 'We must be insane.'

'I'm glad we did,' he said happily, rolling over to look at her, and he smiled when he saw her face. 'Leaving you was the dumbest thing I ever did. And all I've wanted for the last year was a second chance. I never thought it was possible, or I'd have approached you sooner. I thought you hated me. You have every right to. I'm amazed you don't. I think I would have just let this go, no matter how much I still loved you. But when I saw you at La Goulue in New York, I just couldn't. I knew I had to at least see you and talk to you. I've been crazed over you since that night.'

'You wanted a second chance to do what?' She sat up and stared at him, looking angry finally.

'Leave me again? I'm not coming back to you,' she said with a look of fierce determination, as she sprang out of bed, and he admired her long graceful limbs. She had an exquisite body that belied her age. 'We don't even live in the same country anymore,' she said as though that were the only reason not to start their relationship again. 'I don't believe in long-distance romances. And I'm not coming back to New York either. I'm happy here.'

'Well, now that we got all that out of the way, why don't I make us breakfast? And may I point out to you that if you don't come back to me, Fiona Monaghan, that makes you nothing more than a one-night stand, and you're not that kind of woman. Nor am I that kind of man.'

'Then I'll learn to be. I will never marry you again.'

'I don't recall asking you,' he said as he got out of bed, and stood next to her with his arms around her. 'I love you, and I think you love me. What we decide to do about it remains a matter for some discussion.'

'I won't discuss it with you,' she said stubbornly, still standing naked next to him, but she didn't resist his embraces. She had enjoyed the night before as much as he did. 'I thought you were leaving.'

'My plane isn't till four o'clock. I don't have to leave for the airport till one.' The clock on her bed table said it was nine o'clock. That gave them exactly four hours to solve the problem. 'We can discuss it over breakfast.'

'There's nothing to discuss,' she said as she stormed into the bathroom and slammed the door, and he climbed into his trousers and went to make breakfast. She joined him ten minutes later after brushing her teeth and combing her hair, wearing a pink bathrobe.

'Did you steal that from the Ritz?' he asked with interest. He was scrambling eggs and frying bacon, and looked perfectly happy.

'No,' she growled at him, 'I bought it. I can't believe I slept with you. That's the dumbest thing I've ever done. I don't do retreads.'

'That's a charming thing to call me.'

'I could call you a lot worse, and should have,' she said, sticking a baguette in the oven to heat it up, and putting on a pot of coffee. 'This was just plain stupid.'

'Why? We love each other.' He looked calm as he glanced at her. He hadn't been this happy since he left her.

'Would it be tasteless to remind you that you divorced me? And for all I know, you were right. Our lives were just too different.'

'Everything's different now. You're a starving writer, living in a garret in Paris. You could marry me for my money.'

'I have my own money, I don't need yours.'

'That's a shame. If you were after me for my money, everything would be perfect.'

'You're not taking this seriously,' she scolded him, as she took the baguette out, and poured them both coffee. She put the correct amount of sugar in it, and handed him the cup.

'I'm taking it very seriously. You're the one who's not serious. It's totally immoral to sleep with a guy and tell him to get lost in the morning. Particularly if he says he loves you.'

'I don't want a relationship, I don't want a boyfriend, and I don't want a husband. I just want to be left alone to write my book. Look, we did a stupid thing. We went to bed, lots of ex-wives and ex-husbands do that. It's called a lapse of judgment. We did it. It's over. You go back to New York. I'll stay here. We forget we ever did it.'

'I refuse to forget it. I'm addicted to your body,' he said, teasing her as he put the scrambled eggs on plates, added the bacon, and sat down at the kitchen table.

'You've done fine without my body for the last year. Join a twelve-step program.'

'You're not funny,' he said seriously.

'Neither are you. Neither was what we did last night. It was just plain stupid.'

'Stop saying that. It's insulting. It was wonderful and you know it. And do you know why? Because we love each other.'

'We used to love each other. We don't even know each other now. We're practically strangers again.'

'Then get to know me.'

'I can't. You're geographically undesirable. And I know better. John,' she said seriously, holding a forkful of eggs, which were delicious, 'be reasonable. I drove you crazy. You hated being married to me. You said so. You left me.'

'I was scared. I didn't know what I was doing. Your whole life and world were unfamiliar to me. Now I miss them. I miss you. I think about you all the time. I don't want some boring blonde from the Junior League. I want my crazy redhead.'

'I'm not crazy,' she said, looking miffed.

'No, but your life was, a little. Or eccentric at least.'

'Maybe you'd be bored now. I've become very reclusive.'

'At least you're not frigid,' he teased her.

'I could learn to be, if that would convince you to stay away from me. Just take last night as a memory, kind of a goodbye gift we gave each other. Leave it at that. We'll laugh at it twenty years from now.'

'Only if we're still together,' he said firmly.

'I can promise you we won't be. I'm not coming back to you. And you don't really want me, any more than you did before. You just think you do, because you can't have me.'

'Fiona, I love you,' he said, sounding desperate.

'I love you too. But I'm not going to see you again. Ever. If this is how we behave when we're together, it proves we can't be friends, which was what I thought anyway.'

'Then let's be lovers.'

'We live in different cities.'

'I'll fly here on weekends.'

'Don't be silly, that's crazy.'

'So is not being with someone you love whom you once loved enough to marry.'

'And hated enough to divorce,' she reminded him again, and he rolled his eyes, chewing on a piece of bacon. The coffee had been delicious. She always had made great coffee.

'I didn't hate you,' he corrected her, looking mortally embarrassed.

'Yes, you did. You divorced me,' she said primly, finishing her eggs, and looking at him.

'I was an asshole. I admit it. I was stupid.'

'No, you weren't,' she said gently. 'You were wonderful, that's why I loved you. I just don't want to do it again. We did it. It's over. Why screw up the good memories with more bad ones? I had almost forgotten the bad part, and now you come along and want to do it all again. Well, I just don't want to.'

'Good. Let's not. Let's just do the good part.'

'We did that last night. Now you can go back to New York to your friend from the Junior League and get on with your life without me.'

'You just ruined that for me. Now you owe me something,' he said, leaning back in his chair and looking at her smugly. 'You can't just sleep with me and turn my life upside down and then toss me aside like so much trash. What if I get pregnant?'

he asked, looking outraged, and she laughed at him and then leaned over and kissed him.

'You truly are crazy,' she said happily.

'I caught it from you,' he said, and kissed her back, as he glanced past her at the clock and then smiled at her. 'And as long as you're going to just use me and throw me away and forget me, what do you say we give each other a little more to forget before I have to catch the plane to New York? I've got a couple of free hours, if you'll stop talking.' She was about to tell him it was a ridiculous idea, but when he kissed her again, she decided it wasn't. Five minutes later, they were back in her bed again and stayed there for the next two hours.

He got out of bed at noon regretfully. He had to shower, shave, dress, and pick his things up at the Crillon. He had sent his driver away the night before, and told him he would take a cab back to the hotel. He didn't want to keep him waiting. And he had arranged to meet him at the hotel the next day at one o'clock to take him to the airport. He had wanted to walk around Paris in the morning, but liked what he had done with Fiona much better.

'I hate to leave you,' he said sadly, as he put his jacket on. He had no idea when he would see her again, or if she would let him. She was incredibly stubborn, and she seemed absolutely determined to end it. Or not even start it.

'You'll forget me before you land in New York,' she reassured him.

'And you'll forget me even sooner?' he asked, looking tragic.

She smiled at him them, and put her arms around him. 'I will never forget you. I will always love you,' she said, and meant it, and he nearly cried when he kissed her this time.

'Fiona, marry me . . . please . . . I love you . . . I swear, I'll never leave you again. Please help me fix this. I made a terrible mistake when I left you. Don't punish both of us because I was so stupid.'

'You weren't stupid. You were right. And I can't do it. I love you too much. I don't want to get hurt again, or hurt you. It's better this way.'

'No, it isn't.' But he couldn't stay and argue with her. He had to catch a plane. He kissed her one last time before he left, and then hurried down the stairs and across the courtyard, while she stood watching him for the last time. And after he left, she crawled into her bed again, and stayed there all day. At nightfall, she was still lying there, crying, and thinking about him. He called her from the airport, and she didn't answer the phone. She heard him talking to the machine, telling her how much he loved her, and she just closed her eyes and cried harder.

15

Fiona didn't tell Adrian what she'd done when he called the next day to tell her about his Thanksgiving dinner. She listened and pretended to be interested, but all she could think of was John. He had called her a dozen times since he'd left. But she didn't take the calls, nor return them. She wasn't going to speak to him again. She had meant what she told him. It was over. Their night together had been a brief reprieve from a life separate from each other. And in every possible way, it had made it harder. Which made her all the more determined not to speak to him, or see him. She had never loved anyone as she had him, and she didn't want to go through the pain again, especially with him. She loved him too much to try again. And she knew that eventually he'd stop calling.

It took her nearly a week to get back to work. She walked, she smoked. She talked to herself. She tried to work, and couldn't. It was like detoxing from a highly addictive drug. She not only pined for him and longed for him, she craved him. All of which proved to her how dangerous he was for her.

John had been gone for a week when Andrew Page called and told her the second publisher wanted to buy her book. Not only that, they were offering her a three-book contract. It was the first and only good news she'd had since John left, and after she hung up, she realized that even that hadn't cheered her. She felt almost as miserable as she had when he divorced her. And in the last two days, he had finally stopped calling.

She went out to buy groceries that afternoon, which seemed stupid to her since she wasn't eating anyway, but she needed cigarettes and coffee. And as she walked into her courtyard carrying the bags, she heard a footstep behind her. She turned to see who had followed her, and saw John standing there, looking at her. He looked ravaged. He didn't say a word to her, he just walked toward her.

'What are you doing here?' she asked in a flat voice. She didn't have the energy to fight him. But she felt no differently than she had when he left. She had meant everything she said to him, and her agony in the past week confirmed it. He was dangerous for her. She was not going to sleep with him this time, for whatever reason he had come to Paris.

'I can't live without you.' He looked as though he meant it.

'You have for a year and a half,' she reminded him, and set down the bags next to her. They were heavy. He picked them up for her, and stood looking down at her.

'I love you. I don't know what else to say to you. I made a terrible mistake. You have to forgive me.'

'I did that a long time ago.' She looked sad and defeated.

'Then why won't you try again? I know it would work this time.'

'I trusted you. And you betrayed me,' she said simply.

'I would rip my heart out before I would do that to you again.'

'I don't know if I would ever trust you again.'

'Then don't. Let me earn it.' She stood looking at him for a long time, hearing the things Adrian had said to her long before, about compromise and adjustment. She hadn't done it perfectly either. And he was willing to trust her. The only thing she was sure of now was that she loved him.

She didn't say a word to him, she just turned and walked up the steps and unlocked her door, and he followed her in, carrying the two bags of groceries, and he closed the door behind him.

16

The snow was falling on Christmas Eve, and Adrian had come to Paris that morning. He had brought presents for her, and she had a stack of brightly wrapped packages for him, which were piled up under the tree she had decorated the day before. Her apartment looked warm and cozy and festive. And Fiona looked more serious than he had ever seen her.

She was wearing a white velvet dress she'd bought at Didier Ludot, with a little ermine-trimmed jacket. It had been made by Balenciaga in the forties, and Adrian thought he had never seen her look more exquisite. They had booked a table at Le Voltaire for later that night, and they were going to mass at St. Germain d'Auxerrois before that. It was a small, dark Gothic church made of stone, and when they got there, it was entirely lit with candles. She said almost nothing on the ride there, and Adrian didn't press her. She sat staring silently out the window. He took her hand in his and held it.

When they got to the church, John was waiting for her there. He smiled the moment he saw her. It had been complicated to arrange, but John had handled all the details. All their papers were in order. They had been married in a Protestant church before, so they were able to do it in a Catholic church now, which made it feel more official to her. She had told Adrian before he'd come, in case he wanted to cancel his trip, but he insisted he wanted to be there. He was going to visit friends in Morocco when she and John left for Italy on their honeymoon. They were going to spend Christmas together, as planned, and take off on their respective travels the day after. And she had wanted Adrian to be there, as their witness. It still seemed slightly insane to her, and she was amazed at herself that she was willing to do it. She hadn't thought she could trust him again, but she knew she did. And in the end, what they owed each other as much as love was forgiveness.

The priest did the ceremony in French, but he had them say their vows in English, so they knew what they were saying. And as John held her hand in his, and then slipped on the ring, she felt more married to him than ever. There were tears in his eyes when he answered her, and tears rolled slowly down her cheeks as she made her vows to him. It was an unforgettable moment. And when the priest declared them man and wife, John stood for a long moment before he kissed her and just held her. And then he smiled at her with a look she knew she would never forget. When they left, the church was all lit up behind them, and they stood for a moment looking out at the snow, and then dashed to the car, laughing, with Adrian right behind them throwing snow at them instead of rice.

They celebrated at Le Voltaire that night, and at ten o'clock they were home. Adrian was staying at the Ritz, and John said something to him before he left, and the doorbell rang when they were in bed at midnight. John and Fiona were both still awake, and just lying there talking. They had a lot to think about, and plans to make. He was going to commute from New York on weekends for two months, and he had somehow managed to convince the agency to open a Paris office, and he was going to run it. They had to find a house, and he had to sell his New York apartment. She was still trying to convince the owners to sell her the house she lived in, but they were dragging their feet about it. And John had had a serious talk with his daughters just before he flew back to Paris to marry her. He had told them in no uncertain terms what the boundaries were. They didn't have to love Fiona, he couldn't force them to do that. But they had to be respectful, civilized, and polite to her. Or else. It was what he should have said to them two years before.

'Who do you think that is?' Fiona asked, looking worried, when the bell rang. She didn't know a soul in Paris who would ring her doorbell at midnight.

'It must be Santa Claus,' John said with a smile. He looked peaceful and happy as he went to open the door, and a bellboy from the Ritz handed him something. Adrian had kept it in his room for him, and John walked back into the bedroom to Fiona with it.

'What was it?' She was looking at him strangely.

'I was right. It was Santa. He said to say hi to you, and ho ho ho and all that stuff,' and as he said it, he placed the bundle in her arms, and watched her as she opened a small blue blanket and a small black face emerged and looked at her. It looked like a cross between a bat and a rabbit, and she held it to her face with wide eyes and stared at John. It was an eight-week-old French bulldog.

'Oh my God, you didn't . . .' she said as tears leaped to her eyes, and she looked from the puppy to her husband. She set it down on the bed, and saw that it was a little female. 'I can't believe you did that!'

'Do you like her?' he asked, as he sat down on the bed next to her. It wasn't Sir Winston, but it was a distant French relation, and yet another bond between them. He knew how much she must have missed him.

'I love her,' Fiona said with wide eyes, looking just like a child on Christmas. She had bought him a beautiful painting by an artist he loved, but nothing so wonderful as this puppy. And as she held the puppy in her arms, she leaned over and kissed him. She knew as she looked at him that things were going to be better this time. In the ways that were good and right, still the same, and in new and better ways, they would be different. She trusted him again, which was a miracle in itself. And she had always loved him.

'Thank you for giving us a second chance,' John whispered to her, as the puppy licked his face and then nibbled his finger, and he looked lovingly at his wife. The vows meant more to both of them this time, as did the love that bound them.

THE END

RANSOM
By Danielle Steel

A mother's courage, a family's terror, and a triumph
of human strength in the face of overwhelming
odds . . .

Outside the gates of a Californian prison, Peter
Morgan, released after four long years, vows to
redeem himself in the eyes of the young daughters he
left behind. Carl Waters, a convicted murderer, is set
free at the same time. And three hundred miles south
in San Francisco, police detective Ted Lee comes home
to a silent house, while across town, in an exclusive
Pacific Heights neighbourhood, Fernanda Barnes tries
to shield her three children from the panic rising
within her – four months after her husband's death
she faces a mountain of debt she cannot repay.

The lives of these four people come together in ways
none of them could have foreseen. Fernanda, whose
life had once been graced by beautiful homes, security,
success and stunning wealth, encounters a devastating
crime which rocks her family to its core – and brings
Ted Lee into her life. A man of unshakable integrity,
Lee will soon become the one person who tries to
save Fernanda's family from a terrifying fate. Racing
against time in the dark underbelly of the criminal
world, no-one can predict where this overwhelming
challenge will lead them.

0 552 14993 4

CORGI BOOKS

SAFE HARBOUR
By Danielle Steel

*An unforgettable story of survival . . . and of the
extraordinary acts of faith and courage that bring –
and keep – families together . . .*

On a wind-swept summer day, as the fog rolls across
the San Francisco coastline, a solitary figure walks
down the beach, a dog at her side. At eleven, Pip
Mackenzie's young life has already been touched by
tragedy; nine months before, a terrible accident
plunged her mother Ophelie into inconsolable grief.
But on this chilly July afternoon, Pip meets artist Matt
Bowles, who offers to teach the girl to draw – and
can't help but notice her beautiful, lonely mother.
Matt Bowles senses something magical about Pip,
who reminds him of his own daughter at that age,
before a bitter divorce tore his family apart and swept
his children halfway across the world. At first, Ophelie
is thrown off-balance by her daughter's new companion
– until she realizes how much joy he is bringing into
their lives, so that mother and daughter can slowly
begin to heal, to laugh again, and to rediscover what
they have lost. As Matt has to confront unfinished
business from his past, and Ophelie is struck by a
stunning betrayal, out of the darkness that has shadowed
them both comes an unexpected gift of hope.

A story of triumph and a moving elegy to those who
suffer and survive, *Safe Harbour* is Danielle Steel's
most powerful and life-affirming novel to date.

0 552 14991 8

CORGI BOOKS

JOHNNY ANGEL
By Danielle Steel

Johnny Peterson could light up a room with a word or
a smile. He had a future filled with promise – until he
stepped into a car on prom night and, in an instant, it
was all taken away. In the months that follow,
Johnny's family and his high school sweetheart, Becky,
struggle to put together the pieces of their shattered
lives. No-one is more devastated than Johnny's
mother, Alice, but amid the heartache, something
miraculous is about to happen. When a sudden illness
sends Alice to hospital, a glorious vision comes to her
– there, standing before her, is Johnny himself, gently
urging his bewildered mother to be strong for her
family.

Through a season of hope and healing, Johnny walks
by his mother's side, leading his parents, his girlfriend,
his sister and his brother out of their grief. But as
Alice discovers, Johnny has returned not just to help
those he loves, but to uncover a purpose even he
cannot comprehend . . . one that will change them
all forever.

An unforgettable story of loving and letting go –
a celebration of life, hope and forgiveness.

0 552 14855 5

CORGI BOOKS

A LIST OF OTHER DANIELLE STEEL TITLES AVAILABLE FROM CORGI BOOKS AND BANTAM PRESS

13747 2	ACCIDENT	£6.99
14854 7	ANSWERED PRAYERS	£6.99
14503 3	BITTERSWEET	£6.99
14853 9	THE COTTAGE	£6.99
13522 4	DADDY	£6.99
14990 X	DATING GAME	£6.99
14378 2	FIVE DAYS IN PARIS	£6.99
14504 1	THE GHOST	£6.99
14245 X	THE GIFT	£6.99
14508 4	GRANNY DAN	£6.99
13525 9	HEARTBEAT	£6.99
54654 2	HIS BRIGHT LIGHT: The story of my son, Nick Traina	£5.99
14638 2	THE HOUSE ON HOPE STREET	£5.99
14505 X	IRRESISTIBLE FORCES	£6.99
13745 6	JEWELS	£6.99
14855 5	JOHNNY ANGEL	£5.99
14506 8	JOURNEY	£6.99
14852 0	THE KISS	£6.99
14637 4	THE KLONE AND I	£6.99
14639 0	LEAP OF FAITH	£6.99
13749 9	LIGHTNING	£6.99
14851 2	LONE EAGLE	£6.99
14502 5	THE LONG ROAD HOME	£6.99
14131 3	MALICE	£6.99
13524 0	MESSAGE FROM NAM	£6.99
14134 8	MIRROR IMAGE	£6.99
13746 4	MIXED BLESSINGS	£5.99
13523 2	NO GREATER LOVE	£6.99
14133 X	THE RANCH	£6.99
14993 4	RANSOM	£6.99
14991 8	SAFE HARBOUR	£6.99
14132 1	SILENT HONOUR	£6.99
14507 6	SPECIAL DELIVERY	£5.99
14911 X	SUNSET IN ST TROPEZ	£5.99
13526 7	VANISHED	£6.99
14135 6	THE WEDDING	£6.99
13748 0	WINGS	£6.99
05014 2	MIRACLE (Hardback)	£10.99
05019 3	ECHOES (Hardback)	£17.99
05327 3	IMPOSSIBLE (Hardback)	£17.99